Welcome to Lake Vautour

To DeAnna,

Thanks! Enjoy!

Welcome to Lake Vautour

Sarah J Dhue

Sarah J Dhue
2021

First Printing: 2021

ISBN 978-1-6671-3993-7

Sarah J Dhue

www.sarahjdhuephotos.com

Dedication

To my Mom, for her never-ending support and input, and to my editors, Deborah and Max, for helping get this novel from a very rough draft to the book you are holding in your hands. And a very big thank you to all three of them for their support in writing this particular novel; it has been shelved for quite a while, but the time was finally right.

To the many other friends that gave me support during the month of November. Noveling is hard work, and it helps to have people who understand and appreciate that – and also let me ramble about my book's plot.

To Judy, Randy, Emily, Nancy, and Fred, for allowing me to revisit the place where this all began.

To Maeva's Coffee, for an environment which fosters creativity and a very supportive group of employees and fellow customers.

To NaNoWriMo, for challenging me to write 50,000 words in a month. I did it, again!

And most of all, to you, my beloved readers. This would not be possible without all of you!

Chapter 1

Don Lucas drove the car along the winding road, the trees on either side's spring blooms replaced with the lush, green leaves of summer. He was a broad man in his early forties, with dark brown hair and matching scruff. He glanced over at his wife, Beth, in the passenger seat, and she flashed him an eager smile, his dark brown eyes meeting her round, blue ones. Beth was just a few years his junior, with blonde hair cut in a bob.

Don then shifted his gaze to the rearview mirror, where he could see their seventeen-year-old son, Shane, leaning with his forehead pressed against the glass of his window, watching the scenery go by. Shane was almost the spitting image of his mother: slender with sandy, blonde hair and blue eyes, as well as most of her facial features. One of the few things he got from his father was his jawline – and his sense of humor.

This summer was going to be unlike any other that the Lucases had had before. While perusing getaway destinations in mid-January, Beth had come across a place just a few hours away from St. Louis that rented summer cabins anywhere from just a weekend to an extended stay. She had instantly fallen in love with the scenery and then with the cabin that they had listed as available for extended lease.

It was positioned where it overlooked the lake that was the centerpiece – Lake Vautour – and had all the amenities of home: indoor plumbing, electricity, air conditioning, etc. It was a two-bedroom house complete with a full kitchen and two bathrooms. When she'd shown it to Don and suggested making the investment, he'd seemed keen on the idea. While the Lucases were nowhere near retirement, Shane was about to be starting his senior year of high school, and they had often talked about getting a cabin or some form of timeshare once he went away to college, just to keep things interesting.

They had made the arrangements through the website and then told Shane about their plans for the summer. Of course, he was bummed about not getting to spend the entire summer running around with his friends, but after looking at the website, he was excited to explore the woods surrounding Lake Vautour. Shane and some of his friends liked to go on hiking excursions whenever they got the chance; he was not the kind of kid who wanted to stay inside all summer playing video games and binging Netflix. And who knew – there might even be other kids his age staying at the lake.

Now, as he rode in the car with his forehead pressed against the window, the glass cold against his skin and all of his belongings for the next few months packed in the trunk or piled on the seat beside him, his excitement was at a peak, but so was his exhaustion. His mother had woken him at four o'clock in the morning so that they could get everything in the car and an early start on the road. He wanted to nap, but sleep evaded him as they drew nearer and nearer to the cabin that they'd all been looking forward to for almost five months.

Don turned on to a narrow road, and they passed a wooden sign with large, yellow letters that read 'Welcome to Lake Vautour.'

"Here we go," Beth said with excitement, squeezing Don's thigh. "Almost there!" She turned back to look at Shane, "You excited, Shane?"

"Mm-hm," Shane replied, nodding and sitting up. "Just tired."

"Well, the cabin will have your own room with a bed that you can take a nap on… Once we get settled in, of course."

"Of course," Shane bugged his eyes. His mother was the definition of a busy bee; he was sure that if you looked the term up, her picture would be the first thing to come up in the Google search.

"Honey, can you check the map? I know the website said that the turnoff for our cabin could be easy to miss," Don said to her, biting his lower lip and scratching his stubble.

Beth pulled the folded up piece of paper from her purse and looked between it and the road. "Um... you should be close... *There!* There it is!" she suddenly shouted, and Don had to take a hard left so as not to miss the narrow drive almost completely hidden by foliage, causing Shane to bounce around in the backseat; he was glad that he was no longer leaning against the window, or he would've been starting his summer vacation with a nasty bump.

"Easy to miss," Don grumbled under his breath. "Try cutting back some of those damn bushes..." Beth gently patted his shoulder, and he stopped his griping, glancing at her and smiling apologetically. "Not much farther now; this should be the driveway…" he said loud enough for both Beth and Shane to hear.

The driveway was completely enclosed in an archway of trees blocking out almost all of the sunlight. Shane caught a chill and wished that he was sitting up front where he could adjust the AC. The car finally emerged from the cover of trees and into a clearing, the cabin visible farther down the drive beyond a spanning lawn.

Beth let out a subdued squeal, putting her hand over her open mouth and starting to giggle as Don smiled at her excitement. Shane looked out his window and could see the lake farther out beyond the house. It looked almost exactly like on the website but… creepier, somehow.

As they pulled up next to the cabin, there was a tan truck parked outside as well. Shane was sure it had to belong to the forest rangers; his parents had said something about them being there to greet the family when they arrived. As Don shifted into Park, two men climbed out of the truck in tan ranger uniforms complete with badges. The driver was an older man, his head completely bald on top, and what hair he did have was very grey, with thick whiskers to match. His brow seemed like it was probably set in a constant frown, the wrinkles around his dark brown eyes only seeming to confirm that fact. The other ranger was much younger, with brown hair in a crewcut and his face completely clean shaven, not even sideburns to speak of. He had friendly, hazel eyes and smiled as he waved at the car, a complete contrast to his partner.

Don, Beth, and Shane climbed out of the car. "Hello," the older of the two rangers spoke. "You must be the Lucases. I'm Ranger Elton, and this is Ranger Damon," he indicated his young counterpart. "Take it you found the place all right?"

"Yes, pretty well, but you should do something about those plants at the head of the drive; we almost missed it."

Ranger Elton shrugged, "Don't want just anybody coming down the road. Am I right, Mrs. Lucas?" He'd noticed Beth grow uncomfortable when he mentioned other people coming up on the property.

Don set his mouth in a firm line, then decided against whatever he had been about to say. "I'm Don. This is my wife, Beth, and our son, Shane." He extended his hand and shook both of the rangers'.

"Nice to meet all of you," Ranger Elton replied; Ranger Damon smiled broadly and nodded, shoving his hands into his pants pockets. "Now, I am sure that you want to get settled in, but there are just a few things we want to go over with you about the property and general area. Lake Vautour is right down there," he pointed down the slight slope to the lake. "And there's a fire circle and picnic area just up the hill behind the cabin; I can point it out to you when we go around the back. There are several other residences around the lake; some are renters like you, and some live here year-round.

There are trails that go all through the woods, so you may see other people from time to time, but it typically is nothing to worry about – just other residents or hikers. I can get you a trail map, but just over here is the entrance to the main trail from the cabin."

Ranger Elton started toward the tree line, and the others followed. "There is one major thing that I think you will want to know about the woods… There's a flock of turkey vultures that roosts here, thirty or more. They've been calling Lake Vautour their home for centuries; that's actually how the lake got its name."

"It's French," Shane piped up, and Ranger Elton shot him a look; Shane couldn't tell if it was a good thing or not since the man's face seemed to be set in a permanent frown.

He continued to stare at Shane a moment before resuming, "This cabin is the closest to their roost," Ranger Elton stopped walking and pointed down the trail. "They roost about a five minute hike that way, when you take a right at the fork in the path. They won't bother you; some people just get a little spooked when they come to settle in for the night."

"*So many turkey vultures… Why?*" Shane wondered. He looked along the tree line toward the lake and noticed someone moving along the shore: an elderly African American man in a wide brimmed straw hat and torn clothes. "Who's that?" he asked out loud, pointing.

Both rangers looked up, and for the first time since they'd arrived, Ranger Damon's smile shrank. "That's Hoodoo Joe," he answered quietly.

Ranger Elton took over, "He wanders around the woods and whatnot. He's not 'all there,' but he's harmless. He's nothing to worry about; just like the vultures, he keeps to himself and never goes near the house." There was an awkward silence, and Beth was noticeably uncomfortable, just like when Ranger Elton had said that they wanted to discourage people from just coming up the driveway. "Let's get back to the cabin; I can give you the keys and show you around a bit."

They all headed back toward the cabin, but Shane kept looking back at the strange man by the shoreline. *"Hoodoo Joe..."* he thought to himself. *"This place is so weird... and kinda creepy. Way creepier than on the website."*

Ranger Elton pulled a keyring from his pocket, "Here are the keys to the cabin; I can get you a second set if you think you all will ever be coming and going at separate times. The front door faces the driveway, but most people use the back door, which overlooks the lake. The back door sticks sometimes, but just give it a little shove, and it'll come open. Gas meter and water gauge are around here..."

The rangers and Shane's parents continued to the cabin, but Shane hung back, watching the trees where the guy they called Hoodoo Joe had disappeared. He didn't make Shane as uneasy as his mother, but he couldn't help but hope that he did not encounter the hermit while exploring the woods.

He shifted his attention to the lake. The water was dark in some places, but farther out, it reflected the clouds and blue sky. He shielded his eyes from the sun and was able to see a few of the houses and docks around the lake that Ranger Elton had mentioned. He wondered how many belonged to renters and how many belonged to people who lived on the lake year round. Having lived in the city his whole life, Shane could not imagine living somewhere like this all the time. But he was looking forward to the change in scenery, at least for a while.

He turned and headed up toward the house and found the back door slightly ajar with the murmur of voices coming from inside. He walked in to see Ranger Elton showing his dad all of the ins and outs of the Internet router and modem while

Ranger Damon talked to his mom about the wood paneling. She seemed to have calmed down since they'd seen Hoodoo Joe across the lake, which Shane was thankful for; if his mother got fixated on something, she was like a dog with a bone – not willing to let it go without a fight. He knew that if she was too nervous about Hoodoo Joe that she would not let him do much hiking on his own. And if that were to happen, this summer getaway would start to look a lot like a prison.

"It is even nicer than the pictures on the website," Beth gushed, clasping her hands to her chest.

Ranger Damon smiled charmingly at her. "I'm glad you like it so much. It really is a nice little house; showing them to tenants sometimes makes me a little jealous," he laughed.

"That should work for you, but if you have any problems, feel free to call the ranger station," Ranger Elton explained. "Sometimes it's the wiring, but other times it's just the weather causing fits with it all the way out here. We are trying to get them to install a tower nearby, but so far, no luck."

"Figures," Don scoffed.

"Anything else you need our help with?" Ranger Elton asked, joining Ranger Damon where he was still talking to Beth about the cabin. No one seemed to notice that Shane had appeared, or that he'd even been gone to begin with.

"I think that will do it," Don put his hands on his hips and looked around the living room. "Thank you both for showing us around and having everything ready for us."

"Of course; it was our pleasure," Ranger Damon smiled and shook Don's hand.

"What about the trail map?" Shane spoke up, and everyone turned to face him.

"I have one in the truck that I can get for you in a moment," Ranger Elton replied. "Just be sure to stick to the trails; we have had a bit of a poison ivy outbreak this year, and it's all we can do to keep up with the high-traffic areas." Shane nodded eagerly, and the Lucases followed the rangers out to their truck. Ranger Elton opened the driver door and leaned in, stepping back out with a brochure gripped in his hand. He handed it to Shane and managed a small smirk, the closest thing to a smile that Shane had seen on his generally unwelcoming face since they had arrived. "There's your map."

Now that they were outside in the open, Beth seemed to grow nervous again. "Are you sure that Voodoo Joe guy won't come wandering up close to the house or cause any trouble? Like with the car? Or…"

"You have nothing to worry about," Ranger Elton replied. "We have never received any complaints. Fella keeps to himself out there in the woods and stays away from the trails. Chances are you won't be seeing him again." He climbed into the truck, but Beth still seemed unsure.

"You really have nothing to worry about, ma'am," Ranger Damon reassured in a much friendlier tone. That seemed to put her a little more at ease, and the family watched the rangers drive back down the driveway into the cover of trees.

"Well, I guess we should get everything unpacked and get settled into our home for the next couple months," Don said, clicking the key fob and opening the trunk.

~

Shane rolled over in his bed, or rather, the bed in the room he'd claimed as his own. He had to take a moment to orient himself in the unfamiliar space, but then remembered that they had arrived at the cabin; all of his stuff was still piled in the corner. Once they'd gotten everything unloaded from the car, he'd skipped lunch and gone straight to his room to take a nap.

He grabbed his cell phone from where it set on the bedside table and checked the time; it was just after two. He figured he would unpack later that evening; he wanted to explore some while it was still daylight.

He clicked on the lamp on the bedside table and picked up the brochure Ranger Elton had given him, unfolding it and scrutinizing the map. It took a little bit of deciphering, but he managed to pinpoint roughly where their cabin should be on the map. From there, he traced some of the trails with his finger. A piece of him wanted to explore the turkey vulture roost, but he thought maybe he would leave that for another day; he didn't want to check out all of the exciting things right away.

He pulled on his tennis shoes and grabbed a water bottle out of his backpack, slipping the brochure into his shorts pocket. He walked down the stairs to the living room to find both of his parents on the plaid, burlap couch watching the TV, or, as he found out when he got closer, asleep with the TV on. He shook his head and continued into the kitchen; they could watch TV at home, and coming to this nature cabin getaway had been *their* idea.

The kitchen was very rustic, with wooden walls, cabinets, and counters. The stove was an old but seemingly sturdy gas one, and the refrigerator was just about as old, yellowed with age, but seemed to run just fine when Shane opened it up and stuck his hand inside.

They hadn't thought to ask – or he'd still been outside watching Hoodoo Joe – if the water out here was any good. Shane had heard several horror stories about arsenic levels from well water, but then again, you hear all manner of horror stories about anything in the country, or in the city, for that matter. He didn't even know if the cabin got its water from a well; he was just making assumptions.

He turned on the sink and let it run for a moment; the water was clear and not a sick, muddy color with a foul odor, so that was a good sign. He stuck his water bottle under the faucet and took a quick sip. Not bad; it actually tasted better than the tap water at home. He filled up his bottle and walked out the back door, closing it quietly behind him so as not to disturb his parents, but leaving it unlocked for when he got back.

He took the trail map brochure from his pocket again and examined it, deciding where he thought he wanted to go. Somewhere across the lake, he could hear someone hammering and the sound of alternative rock music underneath the hammering.

He looked up from the map and wandered down the slope to the lake shore, where they had their own small, plastic, floating dock. He looked out over the lake, trying to figure out which of the houses the hammering and music were coming from. Several of the houses had much larger, wooden docks, accompanied by decently-sized boats. Shane squinted his eyes and noticed some movement on the dock across the lake and a little to the left. As he focused on it, he could make out a young man bent over either the boat or the dock hammering on something, which made him pretty sure that was where the music was coming from too.

He looked at the map again, trying to see if there was a trail that could get him to that side of the lake. If he was going to be here all summer, he wanted to start making some friends too.

Chapter 2

Shane had found a trail that led nearly to the part of the lake that he was sure the house had to be along and had found a road nearby, following the sound of hammering and alternative rock along the curb. The few other houses he passed were much larger than the cabin he and his parents were renting, and he was sure that the people living in them had to be full-time residents. He hoped that the man he'd seen working out on his dock would want to talk to him; it could be useful to be friends with someone who lived in and knew the area.

Shane stopped in front of the house that the hammering was coming from. He could now clearly hear that the music playing was an old album by the 2000s band *The Frantic*. The house was a nice two-story one, built from pale brick and multi-gabled. The roof appeared to have recently been re-shingled, the shingles a pleasing shade of dark teal that paired well with the pale bricks. The door was set into an archway, dark wood with a heavy, metal knocker. The driveway was limestone gravel and curved around to the back of the house where Shane couldn't see, but could hear the hammering.

He suddenly felt nervous. The house in itself was a bit overwhelming, but he would also have to walk onto the property and out onto the dock out back to approach a total stranger who was probably just trying to work on something. From across the lake, he'd looked like a young man, and maybe he wouldn't have time or interest in entertaining Shane. Then again, Shane was only a few months from being a man himself.

Back at the cabin, approaching someone in the hopes of striking up a new friendship had been exciting, especially since he was going to be here for the whole summer. Now, it just made him feel sick to his stomach. He took the first step onto the driveway, the gravel crunching under his shoe. As he followed the curve of the driveway, the dock came into view, and it was even more impressive than it had appeared from across the lake.

The dock was built in an L shape, one side running parallel to the shore furnished with a patio table and chairs, the umbrella in the center collapsed. The other leg of the dock extended out into the water to where a boat was moored. The boat was an average-sized deck boat that was mostly white with navy blue detailing and had a hard top over the main controls.

The young man Shane had seen from across the lake was bent over the end of the dock hammering, an old stereo and bottle of Budweiser sitting on a wooden bench that was built into the dock. From behind, Shane could see that he was wearing a collared, brown, plaid shirt, blue jeans, and heavy duty hiking boots.

"H-Hello?" Shane said nervously, and for a moment, he was sure that there was no way that he could've been heard over the music and hammering. Much to his surprise, the man turned to look over his shoulder and noticed Shane standing on the border where the yard met the dock. He turned back to his work for a moment and then stood, brushing off his pants and turning to face Shane. His short, dark brown hair was cut in such a way that it was longer on the top and fell into his eyes; he ran his hand through it and swept it back over the top of his head, a few strands still falling back into his face. The lower half of his face was covered in dark stubble.

He reached over and turned down the stereo so that the music was just a hum in the background. His initial expression was one of confusion, but then he smiled at Shane, his green eyes seeming friendly and making Shane feel a little less awkward about trespassing. "Hi there. Can I help you with something? If you're looking for the ranger station to Lake Vautour, it's just–" he started to point up the road back the way Shane had come.

"Er, no, I'm actually staying on Lake Vautour in one of the cabins and saw you on the dock and thought I'd come see what you were working on." Shane instantly hated the words that had come out of his mouth; he felt that he sounded lame, and the man before him was oozing with cool vibes.

"Oh, awesome. When did you get in?" the man asked and then gestured for Shane to come down on the dock, extending his arm to shake hands. "I'm Rosco Ewan, by the way."

Shane approached and shook his hand, becoming more relaxed the more welcome he felt. "Shane Lucas. Me and my parents just arrived this morning."

Rosco nodded and looked out over the lake. "So, you all just here for the weekend, or…?"

"No, we're here for the summer. Which is actually why I came to say 'hello.' Figured it'd be good to start making friends since I'm gonna be here for a while."

Rosco smiled again, taking a swig of his beer. "Well, that shouldn't be too hard; Lake Vautour is a friendly place." He noticed the trail map sticking out of Shane's back pocket. "You into hiking?"

"What?" Shane asked, caught off guard. Rosco indicated the map. "Oh, yeah. Ranger Elton gave it to me. He seemed kinda uptight."

"Oh yeah, he's always been like that. Been working on the lake since right around the time I was born. But he's a good man under all that rough exterior. Damon is friendly too, just still new to the job. This is only his second year here." There was a brief pause and then Rosco interjected, "How old are you? Sixteen, seventeen…?"

"Seventeen."

"Right on," he nodded. "My sister is your age. She should be around here somewhere. She likes hiking too and knows the woods better than any of those maps," he chuckled.

"So, have you two lived here all your lives?"

"Yeah," Rosco nodded.

"It's a great house," Shane turned back to admire the house and noticed the large windows overlooking the lake and a patio with more lawn furniture.

"Yeah, it is," Rosco nodded, growing serious. "It's a lot to keep up with for just me and the sis, though."

"Oh, so she lives with you?" Shane asked, suddenly feeling awkward again.

"Yeah, I'm her guardian," Rosco shrugged it off. "But you're right, it is a great house." He nodded, seeming to become lost in thought.

"What do you know about Hoodoo Joe?" Shane blurted, wanting to change the subject, but quickly regretting it.

"Hoodoo Joe?" Rosco gave him a strange look, pursing his lips and furrowing his brow. "Oh, he's harmless, just been wandering around the woods near Lake Vautour since… forever."

"Why are you two talking about that old kook?" a girl's voice sang out from the direction of the house, and Shane turned to see who had spoken. Coming down toward the dock from the house was a girl who had to be about his age, with blonde hair pulled into two low ponytails. She was wearing a pink, spaghetti strap, tank top, denim shorts, and grass-stained, pale pink Converse sneakers. As she got closer, Shane could see that her facial features were very similar to Rosco's, except for the lack of facial hair and that her eyes were brown.

"Ah, there she is." Rosco grinned lopsidedly and gestured toward the girl, "This is my sister, Kelsey. Kelsey, this is Shane Lucas. He and his family are renting one of the cabins on the lake for the summer. You two are the same age."

"Hi, Shane," Kelsey beamed and scampered up next to him on the dock. He tried not to blush; she was very cute. "It'll be nice to have someone to hang out with on the lake who isn't old as hell or my brother." She giggled, "Not that Rosco isn't cool, but who wants to spend all summer hanging out with their sibling?"

"I wouldn't know; I'm an only child," Shane shrugged; he couldn't believe she was talking about her brother so offhandedly with him right there.

"Oof, that must be boring." Kelsey skipped down the dock and shielded her eyes from the sun, staring out over the lake. "Which one is yours?"

"Um…" Shane walked up next to her and looked out over the lake. He spotted his family's grey-blue Honda CR-V parked next to the cabin. "That one," he pointed.

"Ooo, that's the nice cabin!" Kelsey exclaimed. "I mean, they're all nice, but that's the one with the best view of the lake, in my opinion." She quickly changed the subject. "What do you wanna know about Hoodoo Joe?" She frowned and rolled her eyes, "I'm totally getting ahead of myself;

how do you even know about Hoodoo Joe?"

"Kelsey, go easy on him; he just got here," Rosco urged her.

"Exactly, he *just* got here. So, how does he know about Lake Vautour's most enigmatic resident?"

"Uh," Shane spoke. "We saw him in the woods when Ranger Elton and Ranger Damon were showing us the cabin. He kinda freaked my mom out, but the rangers assured her that he just keeps to himself." Shane bit his lower lip, "Is that true? He doesn't bother anyone; just wanders around being weird and," he circled his index finger around his temple in the universal motion for 'crazy.'

"Pretty much. I wish there was a more exciting story for me to tell you," Kelsey shrugged. "Some people say he sets up camp and brews weird potions and shit, but I've never found a camp of any sort in the woods. Even off trail. You like hiking?" Kelsey snatched the map out of Shane's pocket and gave it a quick glance before balling it up and tossing it over her shoulder, "Pfffft."

"Hey!" Shane lunged to grab the map before it fell victim to the lake.

"You won't need that silly thing. I mean, you won't if you wanna go hiking with me. Could be fun, right?"

"Oh," Shane knew he was blushing now and was thankful he'd chosen to wear loose fitting shorts. "Yeah, that'd be fun. But Ranger Elton said to stick to the trails because of the poison ivy outbreak…"

"Trails schmails, where's the fun in that? And a little poison ivy never hurt me," she shrugged, shoving Shane playfully.

He smiled and managed a small laugh. He flattened the map out all the same and returned it to his pocket, then checked his digital watch. "Oh, shoot!" he exclaimed. "I have to go, my parents will be expecting me back for dinner," he started up the dock back toward the house. "Sorry for just barging in like this, but it was great to meet you two! I hope you'll wanna hang out more while I'm here. It's actually a relief to find other young people here," he laughed nervously.

"Any time. It was nice to meet you, Shane," Rosco nodded, finishing off his beer.

"See you later, Shane!" Kelsey shouted, waving enthusiastically as Shane turned and jogged up the driveway.

Chapter 3

Shane lay in bed, staring at his window and listening to the different noises both inside and outside the cabin. In the city back home, there were always all manner of noises: traffic, people shouting or laughing, sirens… But here it was different. The old cabin seemed to creak and groan, almost as if it were breathing deeply in slumber. Outside his window, he could hear the chirping of insects and tree frogs and the rustling of leaves. He knew some people found it easier to sleep in the country, but he had to say that the 'quiet' was actually making it harder for him to fall asleep.

He rolled over and thought about Kelsey. He smiled to himself, closing his eyes so that he could fully picture her. He thought of her trotting down to the dock – how enthusiastically she spoke. How it was oddly satisfying to hear her cuss. He thought of her stealing the map from his pocket, her hand brushing his hip as she did so. She'd said that he wouldn't need it if he was going to be hanging out with her…

Shane suddenly realized that he could no longer hear the bugs and frogs outside; the night had fallen uncannily silent, aside from the rustling of the trees, but even the wind seemed to have slowed. Shane grew tense; he could not explain it, but he felt as though he were expecting something – as though something were coming.

A piercing yowl suddenly cut through the silence, causing Shane to sit bolt upright in his bed and turn toward the window. His heart was beating out of his chest, and a part of him was overcome with morbid curiosity and wanted to go look out the window, but he kept that part of him in check. Maybe it was just an owl? Or the turkey vultures? Ranger Elton had said that they roosted nearby. But were turkey vultures even nocturnal?

It didn't matter; Shane knew one thing, and it was that he was getting himself worked up over nothing. He was just trying to get used to his new surroundings. The sound probably hadn't even been that loud; it had just seemed loud because it was so quiet outside. As he sat in bed, he noticed that the crickets had resumed their singing; maybe they had just been resting their voices.

Shane laughed to himself and lay back down, snuggling under the heavy comforter on the bed. He was adjusting. A lot had happened in one day, and he had much to look forward to. He decided that when he got up in the morning, he'd talk to his dad about connecting his laptop to the cabin's Wi-Fi and sending a message to his friends back home about what the lake was like and the interesting Ewan siblings across the lake. He finally drifted off to sleep, his dreams filled with images of curving woodland trails, eerie hobo camps, and taking Rosco's boat for a spin on Lake Vautour with Kelsey.

~

Shane awoke to the sound of clanging pans and his mother shouting, "I cannot find a damn thing in this kitchen! I will *have* to reorganize these cabinets!"

"Mm-hm," his father grunted, he assumed from behind the newspaper or some form of manual.

Shane rolled over and stretched, deciding that he should probably get up. He checked the time and saw that it was just after nine – a much more reasonable time than four. He put his feet into his slippers, one of the few things that he'd unpacked and shoved under the bed the night before for easy access. He exited his room and walked down the stairs into the space that functioned as both the dining room and living room.

His father was seated at the table with a cup of coffee, his nose buried in a local newspaper; apparently, his mother had been able to find the coffee, filters, and coffee maker. He could still hear his mother in the kitchen, opening and closing cabinets.

"Good morning," he said, stretching again as he pulled out a chair that faced the kitchen doorway and sat down.

His mother stuck her head out of the kitchen, "Good morning. How did you sleep?"

"Pretty well," Shane nodded, waiting to see if his parents would offer any indication of how they'd slept.

"I think I had the best sleep I've had in months. This getaway is just what I needed," she smiled and inhaled deeply. "The fresh air has done wonders for my migraines." Shane thought about mentioning the weird noise he'd thought he'd heard, but his mother was in such a good mood that he didn't want to spook her, so he decided to keep it to himself. "I'm making pancakes, if I can find all the right utensils. I think I'll spend part of the morning redoing the kitchen," Beth said decidedly, walking back into the kitchen.

When Shane was sure that she was too involved in what she was doing to pay him any attention, he leaned over to his dad and spoke in a hushed tone, "How did you sleep?"

"Like a log," he replied without looking up from the paper.

"So, you didn't hear... any weird noises?"

Don looked up from the paper. "What, like bongos?" he snickered, obviously referring to Hoodoo Joe. He let his joke marinate for a moment and then continued, "No, I didn't hear anything. Did you?"

Shane hesitated, biting the side of his tongue and staring at the grain of the wooden table. After a short deliberation, he looked up at his father, "Probably nothing. I think I'm just adjusting to the nature sounds and the house settling. It was probably just an owl or the vultures."

"Probably was," his father reassured him. "It is a lot different staying out here than it is in the city. My grandparents had a farm when I was growing up, and the first few times I stayed there, I had the hardest time falling asleep because it was just so weirdly quiet that I noticed every little sound."

TICK TICK TICK.

There came a rapping at the back door, and both Shane and his father leaned to look. Through the glass Shane could see Kelsey standing outside, already fully dressed. He suddenly felt embarrassed for still being in his pajamas.

"Who's that?" Don asked.

"Oh, um, a girl I met yesterday who lives across the lake." Shane shot up from his chair and shouted, "Just a minute!" at the back door and bounded up the stairs, taking them two at a time.

He quickly stripped out of his pajamas and pulled on the first pair of shorts and T-shirt that he saw, kicking off his slippers and pulling on socks; he didn't need to wear his sneakers around the cabin. He ran his hands through his hair, but it didn't do much; his hair always seemed to have a mind of its own. He sniffed his armpits and quickly applied some spray deodorant before running back down the stairs and answering the back door.

"Hi," he said, smiling. "Didn't expect to see you so early."

"Oh, sorry. I'm an early riser. Guess I should have texted first, but I don't have your number." Shane blushed, trying to figure out if she was flirting or not. "Do I smell pancakes?"

"Um, yeah. You wanna join us for breakfast?" Shane stumbled over his words.

"Sure! I already ate, but would never turn down pancakes."

Shane led Kelsey into the dining area and introduced her to his dad. "Dad, this is Kelsey. She lives across the lake."

"Hello Kelsey, nice to meet you," Don put down his newspaper and smiled. "I'm glad to see that Shane is already making some new friends."

"Well, you know, Lake Vautour is a friendly place," she grinned, seeming to regurgitate her brother's words from the day before. "You don't mind if I join you for breakfast?"

"Of course not!" Don said enthusiastically. "Have a seat." As she sat down, he shot Shane a suggestive grin.

Shane simply flared his nostrils in response and stepped into the kitchen. "Hey, Mom, a new friend I made yesterday stopped by. She's going to join us for breakfast."

"Oh, a new friend already! That's great; why didn't you mention anything yesterday?"

"Uh," Shane had not thought to mention it because he had wanted to wait and see if his relationship with the Ewans went any further. He had not expected one of them to show up at his back door first thing in the morning. "I guess I just forgot."

"Forgot? Or were keeping secrets?" his mother raised her eyebrows, flipping a pancake in the skillet. "You *did* say it was a she."

Shane rolled his eyes. "You and Dad are incorrigible, you know that?"

Beth simply laughed as Shane returned to the dining table, where Kelsey was explaining to Don where she lived and that she and Rosco had a boat, which seemed to really pique his interest. "And so then Shane just comes marching up our driveway to make friends," she said when she noticed that he was back in earshot, and Shane instantly blushed. "Not that we minded at all – we love meeting new people. It's nice to have another teenager around."

"So, there aren't a lot of other kids around the lake?" Don queried.

"Not really," Kelsey sighed. "Most of them live in town. I only really see them during school. Which I guess is fine, since Rosco practically gives me the run of the house." She started playing with one of her ponytails, "You should come over and meet him at some point; I'm sure he would be thrilled to have someone else to talk to who is enthusiastic about boats."

"I might just take you up on that," Don smiled as Beth exited the kitchen with a platter stacked high with pancakes.

The four ate breakfast and continued to chat. Once they had finished, Shane politely excused Kelsey and himself, quickly filling up his water bottle before following her outside. The sun was already high in the sky and reflecting off of the lake, causing Shane to squint and shield his eyes with his hand. Kelsey marched toward the tree line with purpose; Shane had a feeling that there was a reason that she had wanted to get an early start.

"Hey, uh," he spoke, and she stopped, turning to look at him. "I know it's kind of a silly question, and maybe you wouldn't have heard it all the way across the lake, but I thought I heard this weird sound last night."

"Weird sound like…?" Kelsey let her voice trail off, staring at Shane and jutting out her chin.

"Kind of like a… screech? You hear anything last night or… any other night?" Shane shrugged, feeling more foolish each time he spoke.

Kelsey frowned, thinking. "I didn't hear anything last night, but… I think you might've just heard the turkey vultures. They roost nearby, actually."

"Oh, yeah. Ranger Elton mentioned that yesterday. I just… never heard anything like that before back home."

Kelsey laughed, shaking her head and rolling her eyes good-naturedly and turning back toward the trees, "City boy."

"You say that like it's a bad thing," Shane laughed nervously, jogging to catch up with her. "Can I ask you another question?" Kelsey laughed lightly without giving an answer, but slowed and turned to look at him. "Earlier at the cabin, were you asking me for my number?"

Kelsey opened her mouth as if she was going to speak, but then closed it, grinning mischievously and biting her lower lip. "I might have been. I mean, it only makes sense to have it if you're gonna be here all summer."

"Yeah... Makes sense," Shane nodded, blushing, and then realized that because of Kelsey's arrival he had forgotten to talk to his dad about connecting his laptop to the cabin's Wi-Fi. "*Later I suppose,*" he thought to himself; he was not about to give up the opportunity to spend the morning and afternoon with the super cute girl who lived in the nice house across the lake.

"So, where are we going? I assume you have a place in mind?" he asked.

Kelsey shrugged, but kept walking as they reached the path and entered the shade from the cover of trees. "Oh, ya know, just thought we could wander around, let you get a general feel for the place, maybe even find Hoodoo Joe's camp." Shane stopped dead in his tracks, choking on the water he was drinking. Kelsey looked back over her shoulder at him and snickered, "I'm kidding. But I do have a few landmarks in mind. The turkey vultures have already flown off for the day, but they'll all come back to roost in the evening. You should watch from the cabin; it's really cool, but kind of eerie when they all come swooping down. From over at my house, they look like a bunch of bats."

Shane grinned; he was looking forward to seeing the turkey vultures, especially since Ranger Elton had bothered to mention it during his mini tour. He realized he'd left the trail map up in his room, but he was with Kelsey, after all, and her words echoed in his mind: "*You won't need that silly thing. I mean, you won't if you wanna go hiking with me.*" He felt mostly at ease, all of his apprehension from the night before gone and replaced with puppy love jitters.

He followed after Kelsey, trying to remember what the picture of poison ivy in his old Boy Scout handbook had looked like but coming up blank; he was sure that at some point this excursion would lead them off trail, and he didn't want to start out the summer with a miserable rash.

Chapter 4

Shane sat up in his room; all of the lights were turned out, the only source of illumination his computer screen. His legs already ached from all of the hiking he'd done with Kelsey, but it had been worth it. She had shown him several of the trails, as well as shortcuts – none of which had been overrun with poison ivy, he might add. She had also shown him an old, abandoned barn that was practically falling apart, as well as a few other oddball landmarks that she used to help her not get lost.

When Shane had finally gotten back to the cabin, he'd said good-bye to Kelsey and come inside to the air conditioning, wolfing down half a bag of potato chips and guzzling down another bottle of water. Once he'd cooled down, he'd gone upstairs to get his laptop and brought it down to have his dad help him connect it to the router.

Now, he was sitting in his room, trying to login to Facebook with much difficulty; either the signal wasn't great in his room, or the Internet was simply not working. He leaned back on his bed, stretching his neck and rolling his eyes. He thought about what he would type in the message to his friends if he ever even got the home page to load. He would tell them about the cabin and trails, of course. Just how much he wanted to divulge about Kelsey he still had not decided on yet. And he was sure that they would not believe him about Hoodoo Joe, so he would leave that part out entirely.

He looked out the window and saw the sky already beginning to glow with deep colors as the sun began to set. He'd have to go outside soon if he didn't want to miss the turkey vultures coming in for the night; Kelsey had told him they landed at dusk.

Shane attempted to refresh the window one last time before giving up and closing his laptop, putting it on the bedside table and standing up to go outside. When he got downstairs, he found his parents at the dining room table playing gin.

"Where are you going?" Don asked as Shane headed for the back door.

"Just out in the yard – gonna see if I can see the turkey vultures coming in to roost. Kelsey said the best times to see them is sunrise and sunset."

"Oh, that might be cool to see." Beth laid her cards face down on the table. "Speaking of Kelsey, how was your afternoon?"

"It was fun," Shane replied evasively. He already knew why his parents were so obsessed about him hanging around with her. Back at home, Shane never really hung out with anyone besides 'the guys.' He was just not interested in many girls at his school and too shy to talk to the girls that he was. A piece of him wished there was another teenage boy or two to run around the lake with, but the other part of him felt like some of the weird pressure was off with it just being Kelsey. That, and she didn't have a scary, shotgun dad that he would eventually have to meet.

Don also laid down his cards and stood. "Let's get outside."

The family walked outside and toward the lake, turning to face in the direction of the trees where Ranger Elton had indicated that the turkey vulture roost was. For a while, nothing happened, and just when they were about to give up and go inside, the first vultures flew in from over the lake.

They glided in on dark, feathered wings, nearly silent and only having to flap occasionally. They swooped into the trees, circling before landing out of sight. Shane almost would've called them majestic, but their bald, pink heads took away some of the aesthetic.

"Wow…" Beth said, leaning into Don, who put his arm around her.

Ranger Elton had not exaggerated when he'd said there were more than thirty turkey vultures in the area. More and more seemed to appear as the minutes ticked by, filling the sky with silent flight and the occasional caw as they flew and landed, almost like they were greeting each other after the day abroad.

"I'm glad Ranger Elton told us about them. I can see where it would be freaky to see if you didn't know they roosted over there," Beth stated.

The three continued to watch them as they landed and circled, and some took back off, the cawing growing more frequent. As Shane watched and listened, he realized that the sounds the turkey vultures were making were nothing like the sound he'd heard the night before.

~

Shane lay in bed, finding it hard to get comfortable for different reasons than the previous night. Kelsey had put his fears to rest when she'd told him that the sounds he'd heard were most likely the vultures. Now, he was overcome by a feeling of dread, wondering what had been making them if it had not been the massive, ugly birds.

He had finally gotten the page to load so that he could message his friends, but he'd kept it short and to the point; he was just far too preoccupied about the vultures and the night sounds. He'd told them they had arrived at the lake, that the cabin was neat and there were lots of trails to hike, and that he'd made a couple of friends across the lake. He decided to add in the detail that one of these friends was a cute girl their age.

He stared up at the ceiling, lying on his back because he didn't want to turn his back to the window, but also didn't want to be looking directly at it. The insects seemed to be screaming, the sound pounding against his eardrums, the leaves and branches of the trees rustling in the strong winds that were threatening to bring rain in the coming days.

There just had to be an explanation. Shane was analytical by nature; he always had to find the answer to any problem he was faced with. He was certain that if he just knew what'd let out that awful sound that it wouldn't bother him so much, and he would be able to just let it go.

A piercing screech caused him to sit bolt upright in bed. It was similar to the sound he'd heard the night before, but more... He couldn't find the word, but something about the way the screech had changed sent a chill down his spine. It was followed by a shrieking yowl, definitely made by the same creature, but even more disturbing.

Shane stared at the window, drenched in sweat, his heart drumming in his chest as he tried to regulate his breathing. He wanted to get up and look out, to see if by some twist of fate he would be able to catch a glimpse of what was out there or maybe even see it dart across the backyard. The idea of whatever it was being so close to the house made him shudder and kept him rooted to the spot.

He rationalized that the sound had been fairly far off, so he likely would not see anything. Morbid curiosity took control, and he silently pulled back the covers and climbed out of bed, the wooden floor coarse under his bare feet, but he didn't want to bother with his slippers. The closer he got to the window, the more intensely his guts twisted into knots, and he thought about turning back several times, but he made himself move forward, taking each step on tiptoe, praying for the floorboards not to creak.

It seemed to take him hours to make the nine foot walk from his bed to the window, and when he was one step from being able to see out, he closed his eyes and gulped before taking the final step to the window. He opened his eyes, leaning on the sill and looking out.

The moon was almost completely shrouded in clouds, making it hard to see much of anything. Shane stared at the yard below, waiting for his eyes to adjust. As they did, he was met with the open field and lake shoreline, but nothing moved. And then he noticed – the bugs had fallen silent again, just like the previous night.

He continued to stare out the window and held his breath. He jumped and almost cried out as a new sound cut through the night: a dog barking. It bayed and yelped like a hound on the trail. The other creature replied, yowling, and then Shane could put his finger on what was different from the night before; tonight, whatever it was, was letting out a hunting cry – a disturbingly, almost-human sounding cry.

The dog began to growl between barks, and the unidentified creature let out one more howl before the dog let out a shrill whine, and then both animals fell silent. A few minutes passed, and then he could hear the insects again. Shane retreated to his bed. He lay there for a long time, unable to

fall asleep, picturing a dead dog every time
he closed his eyes.

~

Shane awoke to find that it was raining.
The light coming in through his window
was a ghostly, grey glare, and he could hear
the raindrops hitting the roof. The events of
the night before seemed a million miles
away, and for a moment, he almost
wondered if he'd dreamed them. But the
more he lay there, the surer he was that he
had heard some kind of animal hunt down
and kill a dog.

He shook his head and got up. He was
excited to be here; he knew that his parents
had wanted to do something like this for a
long time and were finally in the financial
situation to do so. When they had told him
that they'd gotten a cabin for the summer,
he'd been bummed out to tell his friends,
but excited otherwise for the change of pace

and scenery. And then there was Kelsey. So, why did it bother him so much?

Maybe it was because his parents seemed completely oblivious to it – which they probably were. He couldn't help but wish that he was too; then, he would be able to enjoy himself without the curiosity and anxiety nagging at the back of his mind.

He got up and went downstairs, walking into the kitchen. He saw a note stuck to the fridge with a small magnet. It was in his mother's handwriting and read: "*Your father and I went into town for groceries to stock the house and a few other things. You should be able to find something for breakfast. See you when we get back. Have fun, but stay safe. –Mom*"

Shane looked around the kitchen and found a box of cereal, but no milk. He poured himself a bowl anyway and sat down at the dining room table, eating a spoonful and crunching loudly. With the rain, he knew that he wouldn't be going hiking, and Ranger Elton had said that the weather could make the Internet coverage even spottier than it typically was. Lake Vautour was great and all, when you could go out and do something. And he'd been a dummy and forgotten to give Kelsey his number – or get her number, for that matter.

Once he'd finished his bowl of dry cereal, he walked upstairs to his room and fired up his laptop and tried to access the Internet. He had no luck, but then again, he hadn't really expected to with the rain and cloud cover. It had been perfectly clear the day before, and he hadn't had much better luck; just sending his message to his friends had taken nearly half an hour. He shut the lid and went back downstairs to see if he could get any channels to come in on the television.

He managed to find a channel that was running the local news and sat down to study the trail map while he waited for the weather report. He'd brought down a pencil from his room to mark and draw in some of the places and landmarks Kelsey had shown him so that he would have a visual frame of reference. Even with all of the hiking they'd done the day before, they had barely explored all that the woods surrounding Lake Vautour had to offer, with several acres of trails, rental properties, and brush.

Shane looked up from the map as the weather report came on. According to the radar, the rain should be cleared out within the next couple of hours, with a chance of showers overnight. That meant that everything would be muddy, but at least Shane would be able to get out of the house; a little mud never hurt anyone.

~

The rain had cleared up as predicted, and Shane's parents were still gone to the store, so he'd decided to go scope out the ranger station; plus, it would be good to know exactly where it was if there was any kind of emergency. And maybe he could talk to one of the rangers about the cruddy Wi-Fi connection.

While Shane was in no way opposed to getting dirty, he had opted to walk the road rather than the trails to the ranger station. The driveway had seemed long once they had turned off the road to drive to the cabin; on foot, it seemed like it went on forever. He'd finally reached the main road and taken a left, if what the map showed was accurate.

Approximately forty-five minutes later, he'd arrived at the ranger station, which was basically a glorified log hut. It was a small, one-story building with a wide awning and crudely painted sign that read 'Lake Vautour Ranger Station.' Below it was a bulletin board right next to the door. There was also a small, public restroom around the side, with one stall for each gender.

Shane started for the door, hoping that they had air conditioning, when one of the flyers on the bulletin board caught his eye. It was for a missing dog. He approached the board to read more details when he noticed another posting for a missing dog. And another… and another. A missing cat. The more Shane looked at the board, the more dizzying it became that there were so many missing flyers. A knot formed in his gut as he thought about what he'd heard the night before. It *definitely* did not feel like a nightmare now. After staring at the bulletin board a moment longer, Shane pulled himself away and entered the ranger station.

The inside was even smaller than it had looked from the outside. There was a shelf lining one wall filled with brochures and pamphlets concerning things to do in the area. There were a couple of wicker chairs and then a counter. Ranger Damon was seated behind it, appearing to be busy, but Shane wondered if he was just trying to give the illusion that he had something to be doing.

He looked up as Shane entered and instantly recognized him, smiling broadly. "Hey. You're the Lucas kid. How are you all liking the cabin so far?"

"Shane," he nodded. "It's a great cabin. But I actually came up here because I'm having some trouble with the Wi-Fi."

"Well yeah, the weather tends to mess with the signal," Ranger Damon stated matter-of-factly.

"I was having trouble with it before the rain came through. I'm just trying to see if I have messages from my friends back home."

"Oh yeah," Ranger Damon smiled knowingly. "And cell reception's not so hot either – without Wi-Fi. I can check the server, but I can't make any promises. When I started working here, Ranger Elton warned me that it could be temperamental."

"Thanks," Shane managed a small smile and turned for the door. What he'd seen on the bulletin board was still wearing on his mind, and he turned back to Ranger

Damon, "Why are there so many missing dog posters out front?"

"Oh, ya know. Area like this, dogs get loose and run off to who knows where," Ranger Damon shrugged. "Nothing to worry about. You all didn't bring a dog, did you?"

"No, we don't have one," Shane continued out the door and almost collided with Ranger Elton. He barely spared him a glance as he walked by, his brow furrowed in concentration as he walked purposefully toward his partner.

Shane almost wanted to stay and eavesdrop to see what he seemed so uptight about, but the look on Ranger Elton's face made Shane decide that he shouldn't push his luck; he didn't want to start out on his bad side. It was his general understanding, from his own observations and what Rosco had told him that Ranger Elton was just generally on edge, so he didn't want to become the object of his annoyance.

As he started back down the road toward their cabin, Shane saw both Ranger Elton and Ranger Damon exit the station and climb into one of the ranger trucks, speeding down the road in the opposite direction.

Chapter 5

Shane sat down on the sofa in complete darkness. It was after midnight, and he'd nearly nodded off several times. But he wanted to see if he would hear the sound again. Being downstairs would actually put him closer to the tree line than up in his room, so he thought that maybe he would be able to hear it more clearly. The night was exceptionally noisy with insects, thankful for the rain earlier that day.

Just when Shane thought he would give up and head upstairs, he heard it – closer than he had either of the other nights. It sounded like it was right outside the cabin, just at the edge of the woods skirting the lawn. With the closer proximity, Shane did not know how to describe it; it sounded less like a bird and more like a mix between a howl and a human wail. All curiosity left him in that moment. He did not want to see whatever was making the God-awful noise; he just wanted it to leave him and his family alone. He wondered how his parents couldn't hear it…

It cried out again, this time even closer, and Shane bolted from the couch. Whatever was out there, he could feel in his gut, was no good. It was on the hunt, again. He grabbed the phone receiver off the wall in the kitchen and quickly dialed the number for the ranger station taped next to the cradle. The phone rang five times and went to an answering machine: "H-Hello? This is Shane Lucas, staying at 507 Lakeshore Road on Lake Vautour. Th– There's something outside that I can hear howling in the trees. I don't think that it's a normal animal – I don't know what it is, but can you please send someone here to check it out?" Another yowl cut through the night air. "There it is again. Please send someone out here; I'm really spooked." Shane hung up the phone, pacing nervously.

When there were no more repeats of the sound or signs of a ranger, he finally went up to his room and lay down in bed, too scared to fall asleep until he finally couldn't hold his eyes open any longer.

~

Shane had woken up early, unable to stay asleep, images of what could've been making the sound haunting his dreams and causing him to keep waking up. He'd finally pulled on some clothes and gone downstairs to wait for the ranger – if one ever came. He had not bothered to comb his hair, and the quick glance he'd taken in the mirror revealed his eyes to be ringed with dark, purple bags.

He'd found Eggos in the freezer and popped a couple into the toaster. After picking at them, he'd sat on the couch and fiddled nervously with the tassels on the throw blanket draped over the back. He practically flew off the couch when he heard a vehicle making its way along the driveway and opened the front door to see one of the ranger trucks pulling up next to the cabin.

Ranger Damon climbed out, unwrapping a piece of gum and placing it in his mouth. "You called about a disturbance?" he said, nodding to Shane and squinting against the sun. He promptly put on his hat to help shade him.

"Yeah. Good thing it wasn't a real emergency," Shane huffed, following Ranger Damon as he walked around to the back of the house and looking out over the lake.

"Sorry; ranger station closes at eleven and opens at seven." Shane jumped as the foot of the hill that led up to the fire ring came into view. A turkey vulture was sitting on the ground, picking at a mangled deer carcass. Ranger Damon couldn't help but chuckle as Shane realized it wasn't some kind of monster. "So, what exactly do you think you heard last night?"

"I don't know," Shane said, disgusted but unable to take his eyes off of the vulture ripping the strips of meat from the bones of the carcass. "It sounded like some kind of animal or, I don't know. It was yowling and it… It didn't sound like anything I've ever heard before."

Ranger Damon nodded, chewing his gum and surveying the immediate area. "But you didn't see anything?"

"No; I didn't even look I was so spooked."

Ranger Damon nodded again, "Well, you are out in the middle of nowhere, and sound carries at night. It can get distorted over distance. You probably heard a coyote or an owl or one of the vultures or maybe even a fox."

Shane shook his head, "No, this was not like anything I've ever heard before." Ranger Damon inhaled sharply, wanting to watch his words. "Look, I know I'm a city boy and all that, but I know that what I heard was not normal. It was wrong, it just–"

"Hey, Shane!" Kelsey emerged from the trees, waving to him; he suddenly wished that he had bothered to comb his hair. "Oh, *hi* Damon. I didn't expect to see you here." Kelsey grinned at him charmingly, and Shane suddenly felt uncomfortable. "Yucko!" she exclaimed, sticking out her tongue as she passed near enough to the deer carcass for the vulture to pause and look up at her, bracing to fly away if it felt the need to retreat. She kept walking, and it resumed its eating.

"Hi, Kelsey," Ranger Damon smiled shyly, looking at the ground and kicking at the dirt. "Didn't expect to see you here either."

"Well, you know me," Kelsey sidled up between the two guys. "I'm always right in the middle of things." Ranger Damon blushed bright red, and Shane couldn't help but feel like a third wheel. He'd thought Kelsey seemed to have a thing for him, but the tension and chemistry between the two of them made him feel like maybe he had misinterpreted. "So, how's the ranger station treating you?"

"Oh, it's, uh, good," Ranger Damon looked up at her and grinned again, blushing even redder, which Shane had not thought possible until he'd witnessed it with his own two eyes.

"So, I take it Ranger Elton is keeping you busy running around and doing all the shit he doesn't want to?" Kelsey smirked, raising an eyebrow.

"Ranger Elton isn't so bad, really," Ranger Damon scratched the back of his head. "But I probably should get back to the station."

"Oh, come on; how much do you really think he's missing you?" Kelsey pouted out her lower lip and gave him her best puppy dog eyes.

Ranger Damon's voice caught in his throat, and he shifted his gaze to the turkey vulture. "I–" he turned his attention to Shane. "I could remove that carcass for you. I have a feeling that Mrs. Lucas would rather not wake up to that."

"Yeah, that sounds like a good idea," Shane replied, his voice strained as he tried to hide how uncomfortable – and frankly, jealous – that he was.

"If you ever need anything, Damon is always ready to serve," Kelsey almost sang, and Ranger Damon walked over to the vulture and shooed it away. He went back to the truck and came back wearing a pair of work gloves, grabbing the carcass by its legs and lugging it to the truck and throwing it into the bed, quickly discarding the gloves with it.

"Well, that's done. If you don't need anything else, I'm going to head back." Shane looked dejectedly at the ground, and Ranger Damon patted his shoulder. "Don't worry about any weird noises; it's probably nothing and really far off, anyway." He shifted his attention to Kelsey.

"Bye, Damon. Don't be a stranger."

"It was good to see you, Kelsey," Ranger Damon tipped his hat to her before climbing into the truck and throwing it in the passenger seat. He fired up the engine, and Shane and Kelsey watched until he was out of sight.

Kelsey turned to Shane, "Anyway… You called the ranger station about the noises? I thought we agreed that it was just the vultures?"

Shane continued to stare down the drive, not wanting to look at Kelsey because he felt spurned and kind of foolish. "It wasn't the vultures," he said coldly. "I watched them come in to roost the other night… And after hearing them and whatever it is again, there is no way that what I heard is the vultures."

"City boy is getting versed in the sounds of nature. I dig it." Shane exhaled out his nostrils and managed a momentary half smile. Kelsey's tone changed, "Hey, what's up? You're acting all weird. Does a strange sound really have you that spooked?"

"It's nothing," Shane shrugged and turned to look at her. "But I am a little on edge... I barely slept at all last night."

"Aw, poor Shane," Kelsey said; Shane couldn't tell if it was real or mock sympathy. "Okay – if you don't think that it's the vultures, then what do you think it is?"

"I don't know... Why don't we go sit and talk?" he pointed up the hill to the picnic table by the fire ring.

"Sure," Kelsey replied, narrowing her eyes at him and examining his face. The two walked up the hill to the picnic table and sat down under the shade of the trees. "All right, let's hear more about this mystery animal that you're losing sleep over."

Shane stared at the table, running his hand through his hair. "After hearing the turkey vultures, I realized that was definitely not what I heard the first night.

78

So the second night, I heard it again and realized while it's a high sound, kinda like a screech, it's more like a yowling. I think I heard it hunt down and kill a dog…" Shane turned and looked out over the lake, uncomfortable from reliving the disturbing memory. "But that's not the worst part," he finally said after a long pause. "At first, I couldn't put my finger on what it was, but something about how it sounds really bugged me. But then I realized what it was; it sounds oddly… human." He looked seriously at Kelsey.

For a moment, she gave no reaction. Then, she burst out laughing, dealing a brutal blow to Shane's pride. When she saw the look of utter bewilderment on his face, she tried to stop, speaking between giggles, "You probably just heard Ranger Elton fapping." She tried to stifle another uproarious outburst. "I mean, no woman has been with him since his wife left him years ago. You know he has to be," she made a suggestive tugging gesture with her hand.

Shane let out a small laugh. "That's a little mean to say," he said, but was still smiling.

"It's fine; he's a mean old turd." Kelsey rolled her eyes, "But he is pretty uptight, so maybe he isn't getting off, though I can't imagine that." Shane's smile shrunk again. "Shane?" Kelsey said, all of the humor gone from her voice. He looked up at her, "All jokes aside, out here it could be anything. It's probably nothing to get worked up over; there's all kinds of night sounds that sound freaky, but they're nothing."

"You sound like Ranger Damon."

"Because he's probably right." Shane sat and stewed a moment, that last comment stinging even though it probably shouldn't have. An awkward silence followed. "Anyhoo," Kelsey finally broke the silence. "Back to the original reason I even came over here."

She pulled a small, folded piece of pink paper from her pocket and slid it across the table to him. He frowned slightly, intrigued, and picked up the piece of paper and unfolded it. Written on the inside in tall, loopy, very feminine handwriting was: "Kelsey Ewan #" and her phone number.

"Old school," he chuckled, hoping that he wasn't blushing as he pulled his phone from his pocket to add her to his contacts. "I can text you mine–"

"Ah-ah," she pulled a blue piece of paper and mini pen from her shorts pocket. "Your turn; out here we do things old school." She laughed. "I figured maybe sometimes I could text you rather than dropping in unexpectedly. But with the service out here, I probably will end up doing that a lot anyway. And because I want to," she winked.

Shane smirked and took the pen and paper. He scribbled his name and then tried to be more meticulous as he wrote his phone number so that it would actually be legible. He folded it up and handed it back to her along with her pen.

"Thank you, Shane," she said sweetly, putting them in her pocket without looking at the paper. "Now, I was going to ask you what you wanted to do today. But I think you should go take a nap." She stood, placing her hands in the back pockets of her shorts and shrugging. "Maybe if you feel better later, I could talk Rosco into taking the boat out," she shrugged. "He never lets me drive it," she pouted, turning and heading down the hill.

"O-Okay," Shane said after her. "I'll text you later… maybe, I guess, if I can get service."

"Sounds good," she said back, scampering down the hill and back into the trees and out of sight. She was probably right; after the roller coaster of emotions Shane had experienced in the short time he'd been awake, he was exhausted enough to think that maybe he could sleep.

~

Shane had gone back to bed and woken up later that morning feeling refreshed. He'd tried to text Kelsey, but had no luck; he had no cell phone coverage, and the Wi-Fi still seemed to be acting up, despite Ranger Damon 'checking the server.'

"We should've exchanged landline numbers," he thought snidely to himself as he filled up his water bottle and started the hike to the Ewans' house. *"That's about as old school as it gets."*

When he arrived, he peeked around the back, but saw no one outside and the boat still moored at the dock. He walked back around to the front of the house and looked for a doorbell. When he found none, he knocked on the door, the sound echoing around the small alcove. It didn't take long for someone to answer the door; it opened, and Rosco appeared in the doorway.

"Hey. Shane, right?" Rosco greeted him with a warm smile, squinching up his eyes as he tried to make sure he'd gotten Shane's name right.

"Yeah, Shane. Is Kelsey around? She said that if I was feeling up to it later that maybe you would take us out on the lake in the boat?"

Rosco's smile shrank, replaced by a confused frown, "I wonder why she would say that; she knows I don't have it running yet. Carburetor crapped out at the end of last season. It's almost there, but not quite. Unless…" His voice trailed off and he lifted an eyebrow. "She was trying to rope you into helping me."

"Oh," Shane cleared his throat nervously. "Well, I'm no good with engines; that's my dad."

Rosco laughed heartily and patted Shane on the shoulder. "Hey, not everyone's a mechanic. Well, I'm sorry that Kelsey got your hopes up. And she's not around at the moment, so she wouldn't have been able to go out with us anyway." Rosco put his hands on his hips and grew serious, "You said she suggested it if you were feeling up to it... Everything okay over at the cabin for you all?"

Shane wanted to ask Rosco what his thoughts were on the sounds, but he didn't want him to think he was a total loser who spooked easy; he was pretty sure that Ranger Damon already thought so, as well as Kelsey to some extent.

"Yeah, everything's great; just didn't sleep well last night." Shane almost believed the lie. Maybe Ranger Damon and Kelsey were right; maybe it was nothing to get worked up about, and he was just letting his imagination run away with him from all of the horror and science fiction novels he liked to read.

"Good to hear it. You should have your folks stop by some time; I would love for us all to get acquainted. Do you wanna come in, since you walked all the way here?" Rosco opened the door wider, and Shane could feel the rush of the air conditioning from where he was standing.

"That sounds great, actually. Thanks," Shane stepped into the house, and Rosco closed the door behind him. He was ecstatic that Rosco wanted to hangout. While he had what he definitely felt like was a crush on Kelsey, Rosco was older and cool. The fact that he wanted to hang with Shane made him more resolute in the fact that he didn't want to make himself seem like a weirdo.

The house was just as impressive inside as it appeared to be from the outside. The entryway had a couple of scenic paintings, the largest featuring a father and son fishing, their dog sitting stoically by. Rosco walked past him and led him through the living room to the dining room, which had a door out to the patio he'd seen from the dock with a large window overlooking the lake. Set out on the table were several stacks of mail and a few boating magazines that were open to various pages about engine types.

"I was just going through some old mail and doing some technical reading before you showed up," Rosco sat down at the table and indicated a chair for Shane. "Ya know: boring stuff," he rolled his eyes and grimaced.

"Yeah, totally." Shane looked out the window at the patio furniture. He'd love to sit outside sometime and soak up the view, but it was just too hot today. That and he had to walk back to the cabin eventually.

"You gonna want a ride back?" Rosco asked as if he'd read Shane's mind. "I know you're a bit of a hiker, but it is a scorcher today."

"Yeah, that'd be nice. Thank you!" Shane was quick to thank him; he did not want to seem ungrateful.

"Don't mention it," Rosco smiled and nodded.

Chapter 6

The next week went by, and Shane continued to explore the hiking trails and surrounding areas: sometimes with Kelsey and sometimes by himself. He left the off-trail excursions for when he was with her. The strange sound he'd heard almost became a distant memory, except for the occasional night that he'd still think he heard it. But he would just roll over and ignore it, even though every time filled him with a feeling of dread that he could not quite explain.

He and his parents had finally made their way over to the Ewans', and as expected, his dad had been crazy about Rosco's boat. They had gotten into talking shop, so Kelsey had given Shane and his mother the 'grand tour' of the house, and they had ended up on the patio sipping virgin mimosas; Shane had quickly realized that his mother was the only one to receive an actual virgin drink to keep up the charade. Upon tasting the concoction, Shane had raised an eyebrow at Kelsey, and she had simply winked.

A couple of times when Shane had come to the house looking for Kelsey, he'd found Ranger Damon's truck parked in the driveway, and he would have some kind of reason – or rather, excuse – for checking in. Shane got the impression that Rosco did not like the ranger coming around any more than he did. Shane had spotted Rosco, who seemed generally reserved but friendly, shooting dirty looks Ranger Damon's way when he wasn't looking, especially if he was chatting it up with Kelsey.

One day while Shane and Kelsey were on one of their off-trail excursions, they emerged from the trees near the ranger station. Shane had been scribbling something on his map, a habit he'd kept as he explored more of the area, when Kelsey gripped his arm. Shane looked up and spotted a white, mud–splattered Jeep with the canvas top rolled down parked outside of the station. In the back, he could see some kind of equipment, but couldn't tell what kind it was exactly from the great distance.

"Let's go check it out!" Kelsey grabbed his forearm and started to trot toward the ranger station.

"I, uh, don't know…" Shane didn't budge; he felt like while Kelsey may actually be curious about whoever's Jeep that was and why they were there, that she was making excuses to see Ranger Damon.

"Come on; it's not like we get a lot of visitors, and they have all that *stuff* in the trunk! Where is your sense of curiosity?" Kelsey fussed, and Shane caved, following her to the ranger station.

As they got closer to the Jeep, Shane could see tripods, lightboxes, and a series of other camera equipment. "Photographer of some sort," he said to Kelsey as she pulled him along the building so that they were next to the door but not where anyone could see them.

"Or maybe someone making a movie. Wouldn't that be awesome?" Kelsey whispered excitedly.

Shane nodded and whispered back, "Why are we hiding and whispering?"

Kelsey gave him an incredulous look. "Because, I don't want anyone to know we are listening – at least not yet. Haven't you ever played spy before?"

"Yeah, when I was like, five."

Kelsey scrunched up her face and then hit his shoulder playfully. He shrugged, and then they leaned in to listen; the door wasn't completely latched. They quickly realized that Ranger Damon wasn't around, or at least he wasn't talking. They could hear Ranger Elton and another unknown man's voice.

"I'm just interested in why so many roost here," the man said.

"It's a good spot – right by the water. They've been here for centuries," Ranger Elton replied.

"Yeah, but there are plenty of lakes that cannot boast such a large or long running flock. I just want a little time to take photos and collect data."

"You don't need any kinda permit, so I don't know why you're bothering me about it. I would rather that you didn't, though; I don't like the idea of someone coming in and intentionally disrupting their environment," Ranger Elton practically growled back.

"Just trying to be polite," the man said, and they could practically hear the shrug in his tone.

Footsteps started toward the door, and Kelsey quickly grabbed and pulled Shane around the side of the building, peeking around the corner.

"And look," the other man said as the door came open, and he and Ranger Elton came into view, "I don't plan to do anything disruptive to the environment; I want to collect good and *accurate* data." He was a fairly short man; Ranger Elton was not particularly tall and even he towered over him. He wore a tan vest over a white button-up shirt and khaki pants with boots. On his head, he wore a white panama hat stained tan with age, his short, brown hair and sideburns visible underneath.

"Mr. Sanford," Ranger Elton said in a biting tone as they reached the Jeep. "So long as you're not littering, destroying property, or messing with the birds, do whatever the hell you want. But I'm not going to lie and tell you that I'm happy about it or you being here."

Mr. Sanford looked at Ranger Elton uncertainly, shoving his hands into his vest pockets, "Have it your way. I'd think a ranger of all people would be interested in learning more about his land."

"That's our cue," Kelsey said, standing and pulling Shane behind her, then walking casually out into the street. "Good afternoon, Ranger Elton!" she sang out, waving.

Ranger Elton turned and spotted her, sighing and barely keeping himself from rolling his eyes. "Good afternoon, Kelsey. Can't you see I'm a little busy?"

"I don't need anything, was just hiking with Shane and thought I'd say 'hello.'" She gave him her most convincing fake smile. "Who's your friend?"

Both men smirked – Ranger Elton more noticeably than Mr. Sanford – when she referred to them as friends. Ranger Elton shifted his gaze to Shane for a split second, then back to Kelsey. "This is Greg Sanford. He's a nature photographer here to study the turkey vultures and why they chose here of all places to roost."

"Nice to meet you, Mr. Sanford," Kelsey extended her hand, and he shook it. "Do you know they're how Lake Vautour got its name?"

Greg opened his mouth to speak, but Ranger Elton crossed his arms and leaned in toward Kelsey. "Mr. Sanford has a lot of work to be doing. Why don't you continue your hike with your friend and stay out of the way?"

Kelsey opened her mouth to protest, but Ranger Elton narrowed his eyes, and she clamped it shut. She turned back to Shane and took a few steps toward him and then looked back over her shoulder. "It was nice meeting you," she said, and then led Shane back toward the road where there was a trail. Once she was sure that she was out of earshot of the two men, she muttered, "Prick," under her breath.

Shane half-smiled briefly, and then spoke more seriously. "What was that all about?"

"Oh, Ranger Elton hates people tromping around that he feels have no business being here. Basically, if you're not paying to be on the lake – rent or property tax – he wants you to stay the fuck off the land." She laughed, almost meanly, "He just likes being in control of everything. Maybe he should've been a cop and gotten a *real* badge."

Shane shrugged, "I mean, I get him not wanting the guy to disturb the turkey vultures, especially since they have been here so long."

Kelsey let out a harsh laugh. "Ex-fucking-actly! They've been here forever! One little nature photographer in a dirty hat is not going to chase them off." Shane harrumphed; she had a point. "Anyway, I am starving. Let's get headed back."

"Sure," Shane agreed, following Kelsey and pulling his map and pencil back out, tracing their progress.

~

"Have you seen that nature photographer setting up equipment near the vultures' roost?" Beth asked as she cooked breakfast, the bacon sizzling loudly in the pan. "Sandboard, I think he said his name was?"

"Sanford. Greg Sanford. I met him yesterday," Shane nodded, leaning on the kitchen door frame.

"Oh, really? When?"

"At the ranger station; I was hiking near there with Kelsey, and he was talking to Ranger Elton about permits," he replied.

"Hmph. Ranger Elton really does seem to have things under control around here. But Ranger Damon is much friendlier," she said, and Shane internally rolled his eyes. He did not truly have anything against Ranger Damon; he'd just become a point of contention for Shane.

"Yeah, Ranger Elton is kind of a codger," Shane laughed, thinking of all the choice names Kelsey had for him. Whatever she felt about Ranger Damon – be it romantic or platonic – she felt just as strongly about Ranger Elton in the opposite way and made it no secret. Based on their exchange at the station the previous day, he couldn't help but feel that Ranger Elton felt the same way about her.

"I wouldn't say that," Beth shot him a look. "He seems more like… a military man. I wonder if he ever was in the service…"

Shane shrugged and left her to her cooking. He went out the front door, something they very rarely did, and headed toward the turkey vulture roost. He was curious about what all equipment Greg Sanford was setting up; he'd dabbled in photography briefly in journalism in high school, but ultimately, it hadn't stuck. That was how he'd been able to identify most of the equipment Greg had in the back of his Jeep.

He turned off the drive and cut through the trees in a way he knew was a shortcut to the roost from his many hikes in the area surrounding the cabin. He exited the brush onto the trail near the roost and continued on from there. He passed a tripod set up along the trail that didn't have any equipment mounted on it yet and heard someone moving in the clearing up ahead.

He entered the roost and spotted Greg fiddling with a camera on a tripod placed in the exact center of the clearing. His Jeep was parked on the grass nearby.

"Better hope Ranger Elton doesn't see you off-roading," Shane said loud enough for Greg to hear, and he looked up, spotting Shane across the clearing.

"Oh, hello again. Kelsey's friend… right? From, yesterday?"

"Yeah, Shane." Shane walked closer so that he wouldn't have to shout.

"That guy was a piece of work. But at least he didn't pull out some rule about 'no photography' or 'private property,'" Greg scoffed, detaching the camera from the tripod and clicking buttons.

"Yeah, he is a little… inhospitable," Shane chose his words carefully. "So, uh, do you have any theories?"

"Hm?" Greg grunted but did not look up.

"About the vultures… why they roost here in such large numbers."

"Nothing solid yet. It is odd, though, just how long they've been here too. There must be some kind of great food source nearby, otherwise they would move on or be more scattered."

Shane felt a lump form in his throat, "Don't they eat dead things?"

Greg finally looked up, a strange look in his eye. "Exactly." He started back toward his Jeep, and Shane followed close behind.

"So, what kind of equipment are you using? I did a little bit of photography in high school. Nice lightboxes."

"Canon. Thanks," Greg grinned, digging through the things in the back. "Journalism?"

"Yeah; Canons were what they had for us to use in class."

"That was the class that settled it for me – what I wanted to be. That, and my dad's Nat Geo collection."

Shane smiled and then stood awkwardly by for a moment. "Well, I should head back. My mom probably has breakfast ready. It was nice to actually meet you and see some of what you're doing." Shane started back toward the cabin and then looked back over his shoulder. "They'll be coming in to roost at dusk. It is really something."

"I am sure it is. Thanks again, Shane."

Chapter 7

Shane walked out to the roost clearing again for what had to be the twentieth time in the past four days. There was still no sign of all of the equipment that he'd seen Greg Sanford setting up just a few days prior, and he was sure that he had not collected all of the data he needed yet.

After their initial chat about the vultures and photography, Shane had gone out to the roost clearing the following day to check on Greg's progress, only to find all of the nature photographer's things gone. While Shane felt like Greg would've left his equipment set up to monitor the vultures' night activity, he thought that perhaps he had just come out too early. He had checked back again in the afternoon and still, there was no sign of Greg or his gear. For the next few days, he had continued to check back, only to find the clearing empty.

It was strange and bothered Shane in a way that made him feel sick to his stomach; it was almost as if the man and his equipment had never been there. Greg had seemed so emphatic about his research that it felt wrong for him to have just packed up and left so soon. When Shane had tried to voice his concern to Kelsey, she had just blown him off. *"He probably just realized that there really was nothing exciting to see and packed up for a better gig."* That just didn't feel right to Shane, but he decided not to push it with her.

He skimmed his map before folding it and placing it in his pocket. Maybe Greg had just moved his gear to a new location. Or he'd tripped or fallen and gotten hurt, but no one knew where he was. That still did not explain why his Jeep didn't seem to be parked anywhere nearby, but Shane also knew that he had seen him off-road with it, so anything was possible.

He walked on, looking around the trees and at the ground as he did so.

Occasionally, he stopped to listen, but did not hear anything besides the rustle of the leaves and his own breathing.

He reached an intersection of trails and decided to take the one that went even deeper into the woods, as well as in a direction that he had not explored as heavily on his own or with Kelsey. He walked for so long that he lost track of time and was about to turn back when he noticed something just to the side of the trail.

He froze, suddenly apprehensive. He took a few deep breaths and slowly approached it, kneeling. It was a black Canon DSLR camera – from the looks of it, the very same one that he'd seen Greg using just a few days ago; he recognized the button configuration. He reached out and picked it up, turned it so that he was looking at the front, and noticed that the lens was cracked. Not only that, but upon closer inspection, it seemed to be splattered with blood.

Shane's heart began to pound harder in his chest as he looked around for any other signs of the nature photographer, but found none. He pressed the power button and was surprised when the camera powered on; he'd been sure that it'd probably be dead after sitting out in the forest for a while, quite possibly days.

He clicked a few buttons until he found the right one to review the photos on the memory card; this camera was much more complicated than the model that he'd used in school. The first several photos were of the trees where the vultures roosted, followed by some of them coming in to land for the night. After that were a few of different sections of the trail. The following photos were blurred, but Shane thought he could make out what seemed to be several piles of bones and carcasses.

As he squinted down at the screen, trying to make out details in the photos, he heard a noise farther down the trail. He quickly powered off the camera, overcome with a feeling of unease. He held onto the camera and began back down the path the way he had come, back toward the roost and the cabin.

He could hear the crunch of something walking on the dirt and branches snapping as something displaced them nearby; he could not tell from what direction the sounds were coming, but he quickened his pace nonetheless. He rounded a corner and came face to face with Ranger Elton.

Both of them came to an abrupt halt, startled by the sudden appearance of the other. Shane let out a small cry and inwardly berated himself for being so jumpy.

"Didn't expect to see you out here," Ranger Elton said, quickly regaining his composure. "But then again, you did seem keen on hiking." He shifted his gaze to the camera in Shane's hand. "That your camera?"

Shane's heart continued to pound in his ears and the feeling of unease he felt was growing by the second. "Yeah," he lied, trying to hold the camera so that the cracked, bloody lens was hidden from sight.

Ranger Elton put his hands on his hips and looked out into the trees, sighing heavily. When he turned back to Shane, his tone was filled with disappointment, "Thought I dropped mine out here; was hoping you'd picked it up…" He let his voice trail off, looking around at the trees again. "How do you like Lake Vautour?"

"It's nice," Shane felt terribly awkward, since in his experience and understanding from others, Ranger Elton was not one to make small talk. "Except for the disturbances."

Ranger Elton looked seriously at Shane, stroking his beard. "Damon mentioned you called about a disturbance; thought you heard some kind of weird animal." He set his jaw, putting his hands back on his hips, nodding decidedly. When he spoke, his voice sounded distant, as if his mind were elsewhere, "Sound carries at night… Maybe I didn't drop it here." He turned to go, but stopped after a few steps and looked back over his shoulder at Shane, "Stay safe out here, and stick to the trails."

Shane tried to smile, but could feel how fake it looked, and nodded. Ranger Elton returned an equally bogus smile and then continued down the trail. Shane waited several minutes until he was sure that Ranger Elton was gone. Then, he ran as fast as he could back to the cabin.

~

Shane had heard the yowling in the night again; he'd started to hear it almost every night, only this time it always seemed to be closer than it had in the past. He'd found it difficult to sleep, between the night sounds and the camera that was sitting on his desk across the room. He'd reviewed the photos again and, still, the only thing that he could come up with that the photos' subjects looked like were piles of carcasses, their bones visible as they had been almost picked clean.

Shane thought back to his and Greg's talk about how turkey vultures feed on dead things. If the photos were of heaps of carcasses, then that could easily be a food source for them. But it also raised the question of how and why they had gotten there. And what was Greg's camera doing out in the middle of the woods with a broken lens and blood on it?

"Shane," his mother said tentatively. "You've barely touched your food."

Shane snapped out of his thoughtful daze and looked down at his plate where he had been absently moving his food around with his fork. He hadn't even realized that he'd been doing it.

"Oh, sorry," he chuckled nervously, sitting up straighter in his chair and taking a bite, even though he wasn't hungry.

"Everything okay?" Beth asked, watching him chew and swallow.

Shane bounced his leg nervously under the table as he decided whether or not to tell his parents about the camera and what was on his mind; his father had lowered the paper and was also paying attention to him now. Shane set down his fork and leaned forward. "Either of you notice that Greg Sanford has just vanished?"

"Who?" Don asked, furrowing his brow as he sipped his coffee.

Shane turned to look at his mom, "That nature photographer… who was setting up equipment in the roost." She nodded in recognition, and he continued, "He hasn't be around for a few days… At all, really, and all of his equipment is gone."

"He probably packed up and left," Don shrugged. "Or moved to a different location."

Shane shook his head, "No, but that's just it. He was here to research the vultures, so why wouldn't he be in the roost area? And I think I found one of his cameras while I was hiking yesterday."

Shane looked between his parents and then continued. "It looks like he may have dropped it; the lens was broken and there were some weird photos on it. I have it up in my room, I can show you–"

"Shane," Beth sighed. "I know it's been different being away from home for the summer, but I thought you were finding plenty to do and enjoying running around with your friend, Kelsey. You don't need to go making up stories."

Shane stared at her in shock, his mouth agape. He couldn't believe what he was hearing. "What? I'm not making it up; I can show you!"

"Listen," Don looked seriously at Shane. "If you really did find that guy's camera, you should turn it in to the ranger station. The pictures on it are really none of your or our business."

"But if you will just listen; the pictures were of a bunch of carcasses–"

"Shane, that is enough! We're eating!" Beth shot daggers at him, and Shane stopped talking. He took a few more bites of his food and then stood up from the table, practically stomping up the stairs.

"Where are you going?" Don shouted up after him.

"Out!" Shane yelled back, pulling on his tennis shoes and shoving his map in his pocket before coming back down the stairs and going out the back door.

"Shane…" Beth said after him, but he'd already closed the door and headed for the trails.

Shane shook his head angrily as he pulled out his map and looked at it. He'd never seen the piles of carcasses – or whatever they were – before, so they had to be in a section of the forest that he hadn't been to and mapped out yet. He examined his map and assessed the large area in the upper right corner that was as yet unknown to him. There weren't many trails that went that way, but there was the one that he'd started on the day before when he'd found the camera.

Something was amiss; he could just feel it, and he was going to find a way to prove to his parents that he wasn't just homesick and making up stories. And he did not *want* to turn the camera over to the ranger station; something had compelled him to lie when Ranger Elton had asked if it was his camera.

He entered the roost clearing and shuddered. It just felt freakishly empty and quiet. He hurried through the clearing and down the path toward where he'd found the camera. When he reached the intersection, he took the trail that led deeper into the woods. He stopped when he reached roughly the spot he thought he'd found the camera and knelt down, digging through the weeds to see if he could find anything else that would indicate that Greg had come this way, but he found nothing.

Shane stood and continued down the trail. It was early enough in the morning that it wasn't too terribly hot outside yet, especially for late June, and the shade from the trees made his hike a truly pleasant one. He was lost in the scenery when he noticed a movement farther up the trail and deeper into the trees on his left. He crouched down and walked more slowly, trying to see who or what it was through the brush without being spotted himself.

He saw the large straw hat before he saw the man. Shane gasped: Hoodoo Joe! He knew that the rangers had assured them that he was harmless, but being alone with him in the middle of the woods still made all of Shane's hair stand on end. Despite his curiosity and need to prove to his parents that he wasn't making things up, he decided that it was best to slip away unseen. He turned and took a few steps down the trail, hoping that the sound of his shoes wouldn't be enough to alert Hoodoo Joe to his presence. He watched for twigs and leaves, sidestepping when he needed to.

"Hey, you dere!" a scratchy voice with a Cajun drawl called out from behind him, and Shane ducked down, sitting perfectly still. "I see you ova dere. No use tryin' to hide; I have to hunt out here. I have da eyes and ears of a fox." Shane squinted his eyes closed, hoping against all odds that if he just didn't answer that the hermit would just go away. "Come on!" A rock came flying through the air and hit the ground no more than a foot from Shane. "Don't make me throw anotha one; I will hit you dis time."

Shane opened his eyes and slowly stood, turning to face Hoodoo Joe, who stood several yards away in the brush. He slowly raised his hand and waved.

"Now dat's betta," Hoodoo Joe nodded, and as he spoke, Shane could see that he was missing several of his teeth. "Come on ova here so we can talk. I'll lead da way." He gestured with his arm for Shane to come.

Feeling that he had no choice, Shane slowly approached the hermit. When he was a couple of yards away, Hoodoo Joe looked him up and down and let out a light, wheezy cackle. "Well *cher*, you *are* a handsome young fella. Come on; let's get back to my camp. We can sit dere."

Shane reluctantly followed and was relieved to find that the camp wasn't far. It was nothing much, just a small fire, a worn log that acted as a bench, and a small, makeshift tent. Hoodoo Joe lowered himself onto the log and patted the spot next to him. Shane sat down, but left a couple of feet between them. When Hoodoo Joe turned to look at him at such close quarters, Shane was startled to see that he had one white eye and one that was so dark brown that it looked almost black.

"What you doin' so far out in da woods alone?" he asked, pulling a couple of berries from his pocket and tossing them in his mouth, chewing loudly.

"Just hiking," Shane shrugged.

Hoodoo Joe let out another wheezy laugh. "I know you and dat girl have been hikin'. Don't nobody come hikin' out here. And you was lookin' for somethin'." He turned to look directly at Shane, his mismatched eyes boring into him.

Shane looked back, assessing the situation. While he felt terribly uncomfortable being alone with him in the woods, Hoodoo Joe might just be crazy enough to humor him, or at least hear him out. "Does anything… *strange* ever happen out here in these woods?"

Hoodoo Joe exhaled out his nostrils, grinning toothlessly at Shane. "What you mean, *cher*?"

Shane took a deep breath before continuing. "Sometimes at night, I hear this creature crying out… It's like nothing I've ever heard before. Somehow, it just feels wrong – bad – like it's on the hunt. And the worst part is that while it sounds like some kind of animal… it sounds a little bit human too." Shane looked at Hoodoo Joe, trying to read his expression. "You ever heard anything like that, or know what it might be?"

Hoodoo Joe squinched up his white eye and wet his lips with is tongue. "I've lived out here in dese woods for a long time and have heard and seen all kindsa things. Lake Vautour is a friendly place in da day, but it is a completely different matta at night."

"So, you've heard it?" Shane said, perking up.

"I've heard somethin' like you describe, yes. Just what it is…" he shrugged. "Who can say?"

"Wait though; you said you've lived out here for a long time. That means it's not something normal, like a fox or coyote or…" His voice trailed off.

"No."

Shane wasn't sure if this was a good or bad thing, but he was beginning to become more comfortable in the hermit's presence. Maybe it was because he was the first person to take him seriously. "Kelsey, the girl you mentioned you know I've been hiking with…"

"I seen you," Hoodoo Joe interjected.

"Oh," Shane paused a moment, mildly uncomfortable again; he could not remember ever having seen Hoodoo Joe during any of their excursions. "Well, she didn't really believe me when I said what I heard. Nobody has: not my parents, not Ranger Damon."

"Dat boy barely knows up from down," Hoodoo Joe harrumphed at the mention of Ranger Damon.

Shane laughed lightly. "I really wish I knew what it was, though... For a while, I thought it was just the turkey vultures. Makes more sense than Ranger Elton jerking off because his wife left him," Shane laughed guiltily. "That wasn't my theory; it's fucking stupid."

Hoodoo Joe scowled at Shane, "Who told you his wife left him?"

Shane looked back at him, his smile shrinking and his laughter dying in his throat. "Kelsey did."

"Pfft. Well, she lied to you, *cher*. His wife didn't leave him; she went missin'."

He paused for dramatic effect; it worked – Shane was hooked. "Ranger Elton was workin' da night shift at da ranger station. When he got home, he found da house in shambles; it looked as if dere had been a struggle. Da window was shattered, and his wife was gone.

"Dey found no prints, no trace of who had been dere or what'd happened. Dey had no idea on motive. Dey neva found her… and dat was twenty-four years ago."

Shane sat in silence for a moment, thinking. He could not come up with a reason why Kelsey would've lied to him about Ranger Elton's wife. Then again, maybe she'd just wanted to get her jab in since there was such animosity between the two of them. "Is there any chance that she could've staged the whole thing and run off?"

Hoodoo Joe shrugged, "Who can say?"

"But you don't think that's what happened?"

Hoodoo Joe shrugged again.

"Did you see that nature photographer who was here to study the vultures? Greg Sanford?"

Hoodoo Joe nodded, "Yes, I seen him. Set up all dat equipment in da clearin'. Later saw him runnin' down da trail like da Devil himself were chasin' him."

A lump formed in Shane's throat. "W-When did you see him running?"

"Few days ago. Haven't seen him since."

"I think he's gone missing. I found his camera; the lens was broken, and it had some of what I think was blood on it." Shane watched Hoodoo Joe carefully, "There were some pictures on it of what looks like a bunch of carcasses. Is that what the turkey vultures eat?"

Hoodoo Joe thought a moment, then answered, "Vultures eat dead tings, so would make sense. But why would dere be piles of bodies? It would be quite a stink." He waved his hand in front of his nose.

"Guess you're right," Shane chuckled and stood. "Well, I should get back. It was nice to meet you. Thank you for listening to me." Shane almost offered to shake Hoodoo Joe's hand, but then thought better of it.

"I will be seein' you again, *cher*, I'm sure." Hoodoo Joe tipped his hat to Shane as he turned to make his way back to the trail.

When he reached the edge of the camp, he looked back over his shoulder. "Can I ask you one more question?" Hoodoo Joe shrugged. "Do you ever cook up potions here in your camp?" A long moment of silence followed, and then Hoodoo Joe burst out laughing, slapping his knee and beginning to cough from the intensity of his outburst. Shane harrumphed and smiled; his reaction had more than answered him. He turned and continued to the trail.

"Dat girl has been fillin' your head with all kindsa stories," Hoodoo Joe laughed between coughs, still slapping his knee.

Shane continued to smile as he reached the trail and regained his bearings. He pulled out his map and debated if he'd mark Hoodoo Joe's camp, since he knew that he didn't stay put in one place from what he'd heard. He chose to label it lightly in pencil, with a small question mark next to it.

While the hermit might be a little cuckoo, he had at least listened to him and taken him seriously. And he lived in the woods, meaning that he saw and heard a lot more than people might think. Even Shane had been unaware of him watching him and Kelsey hiking. He thought back to what he'd said about seeing Greg seemingly running from something. A chill ran down his spine, causing him to shiver even in the steadily heating up afternoon.

He debated if he should go farther down the trail, but decided that he could do that another day; if there really were piles of carcasses lying around, they weren't going anywhere. And as Hoodoo Joe said, they would be giving off quite a stink if they were nearby.

He felt like he'd had enough excitement for one day, and Kelsey might be looking for him. He knew that he'd have some questions for her when he saw her. He started back toward the cabin with a new spring in his step; he may not have found what he was looking for, but he'd learned some new information and possibly gained an ally.

Chapter 8

"You went into his camp with him? *Alone!?*" Kelsey leaned across the picnic table, her arms crossed and her eyes wide.

"Well, I mean, everyone says he's harmless," Shane shrugged nonchalantly.

"Yeah, that's because nobody bothers the guy. You can't provoke someone if you leave them alone." She leaned back, her jaw clenched; she was visibly shaking.

"Look, he invited me to talk." He decided to leave out the part where Hoodoo Joe had threatened to brain him with a rock if he did not comply. "And he was actually quite pleasant to talk to. Had some insight into some things…" Shane began to fiddle with the zipper on his shorts pocket.

"Oh yeah, like what?"

"Like Ranger Elton's wife didn't leave him."

Kelsey rolled her eyes, "Like that even matters. I was just making a joke anyway.

Wouldn't *you* leave? I mean, look at him: ugly and an asshole."

Shane pursed his lips and sighed. "Yeah, well ya know how Greg Sanford has just kinda disappeared into thin air? Hoodoo Joe said he saw him running through the woods like something was chasing him right before he vanished."

"Shane, look," Kelsey reached across the table, resting her hand on his forearm. "The guy is nuts. I wouldn't put too much stock in what he says. I'm telling you, Greg just packed up and left because he was bored. I know I always am."

Shane took a moment to digest that last comment. "You think I'm boring?"

Kelsey rolled her eyes and sighed dramatically. "Not you; you're one of the most exciting things happening in this place."

"More exciting than Ranger Damon?" Shane breached the subject he'd been avoiding for weeks.

Kelsey looked at him, studying his face and scoffed. "Shane, really? He is like, in his twenties. That is like Rosco's age – gross."

Shane wanted to push harder, but decided to drop it. "Anyway, enough about Hoodoo Joe. Wanna see those pictures?"

"Didn't you say that they're blurry?"

"Yeah."

"Then no, not really." Kelsey stretched, grabbing her ponytails and running her hands along the length of them, moving them so that they ran over the front of her shoulders instead of resting on the back of her neck.

"What would you rather do, then?"

"Something fun," she stated, sitting up straighter and smiling impishly.

~

Shane walked downstairs from his room to the kitchen and opened up the pantry. The top few shelves were lined with food: canned goods, cereal, pasta, etc. He knelt down to the lower shelves where they stored things like trash bags and cleaning supplies. In the back corner on the floor was his father's toolbox.

Shane shifted a few things and pulled it to the front of the pantry so that he could see it in the light. He opened the lid and removed the top section. Underneath, he found what he was looking for.

He pulled out a heavy duty flashlight and clicked the switch off and on to make sure that it had working batteries, which it did. The flashlight was over a foot in length and felt heavy in his hands, the metal body cold from being stored away.

Shane closed the toolbox and shoved it back into the corner of the pantry and stood, closing the doors and going back up to his room. When they'd arrived at the cabin several weeks ago and Shane had first heard the creature, he had been terrified to even look out the window. As time had worn on, he'd grown increasingly curious about what was roaming out there. Greg Sanford's apparent disappearance and the fact that no one else seemed to care or want to take him seriously had only fueled that curiosity.

The final straw had been Hoodoo Joe. Not only had he listened to him, he had confirmed that there was something out there and that something had likely happened to Greg. Back up in his room, Shane brandished the flashlight and swung it like a bat. He was going to go out there tonight and see if he could find any sign of what he'd been hearing.

He had laid some ground rules for himself: To have the flashlight on at all times – it was also big and heavy enough to potentially be used as a weapon if the occasion arose. And to not go too far from the cabin so that he could get to shelter quickly if he needed to.

The sun was just beginning to set, and even though he wouldn't be going out until he was sure that his parents were asleep, he could already feel adrenaline pumping through him. While he was still scared of what could be lurking out there, he knew that if he could find even a partial explanation to just one of his questions that it would put his mind at ease.

~

Shane checked the time on his bedside clock. It was just after nine-thirty, and he'd heard his parents go to bed just after nine. He hadn't heard voices or either of them leave to go to the bathroom, so he was sure that they were asleep. He reached under his pillow and felt the flashlight, pulling it out and throwing back the covers to reveal that he was fully clothed. He picked up his tennis shoes from the floor; he would put them on downstairs – he didn't want to risk his parents hearing him. He was sure they would not approve of this late night venture, whether they believed him or not.

Once he was downstairs, he pulled on his shoes and stepped out the back door, making sure to leave it unlocked. The air was cooler than he'd expected and sent a shiver down his spine. Shane switched on the flashlight and headed for the trail that led to the vulture roost clearing.

~

Ranger Damon sat behind the counter in the ranger station. He yawned, struggling to keep his eyes open. He did not typically work the night shift, but Ranger Elton had said that he had some things to take care of, so he would need Ranger Damon to just sit there and answer the phone if it rang, which at this hour, it probably wouldn't.

Ranger Damon picked up a pen and started twirling it between his fingers. He continued to do so as he leaned back in his chair and stared up at the ceiling, exhaling heavily. He closed his eyes and had almost dozed off when he heard someone walking along the side of the building outside. His eyes flew open and he sat straight up, dropping his pen on the desk.

"Hello?" he said, pausing to listen for a response, but none came; even the footsteps had ceased. He waited for a few more seconds and then scooted his chair closer to the desk. "Probably just an animal," he muttered to himself. A few more moments passed, and he'd almost completely convinced himself that it was nothing when he heard it again, and this time, he could definitely tell that it was the scuffle of shoes.

He let out a loud, raspy sigh and stood, taking his flashlight from his belt as he walked to the door. "Hello?" He stepped out the door and shined his flashlight both ways along the front of the building. "Who is out there?" he asked louder, walking to the side of the building where he'd heard the footsteps. "Look, I'm not in the mood for pranks," he turned the corner and shined his flashlight along the side of the building to find no one and nothing there.

He stared at the empty space for a moment and then shook his head. "Guess it was nothing."

THWAP!

Just as he'd started to turn back, something hit him hard across the back of the head, sending him sprawling face first to the ground. His flashlight bounced across the ground, landing so its beam illuminated his unconscious face. His assailant picked up the flashlight and shut it off, slipping it into their pocket before grabbing him by his ankles and dragging him off into the forest.

~

Shane walked along the trail with his flashlight pointed in front of him. He was having trouble keeping the beam steady because he was shaking, despite his best efforts. He was tense with apprehension, taking each step carefully, all of his senses heightened to detect any movement or sound.

After waiting around in the turkey vulture roost for quite some time and hearing nothing, he'd decided to take the trail that ran along the lake; it was a straight shot back to the cabin, and he was moving so slowly that he hadn't gone very far. He froze as he heard a sound – the snap of a twig. He stood perfectly still, trying to listen, but the sound of his heart beating in his ears distracted from any external noises. He also realized that he was breathing heavily and tried to calm himself down. The sound had come from farther down the trail.

He crept along the trail, using both hands on the flashlight, ready to swing if necessary. He came to a section of the trail that opened up to the lake shore – a place where people who didn't have a dock would launch and ground their canoes or kayaks. He froze when he noticed something lying on the ground.

Shane slowly lifted the flashlight beam so that it fell on what was lying in the canoe launch. He recognized the tan uniform immediately: it was one of the rangers, Ranger Damon from the looks of the person's brown hair. He appeared to be unconscious. Shane took a few steps toward him and circled him so that he could see his face. It was definitely Ranger Damon, and he was out cold. Shane noticed with some alarm that he appeared to have blood running out of his right nostril and ear.

"Ranger Damon?" he said quietly, taking a few more steps toward him and moving the flashlight along his body. As he moved it back up to his face, he noticed a wound near the base of his skull just below his right ear. Someone had knocked him out and left him here… But who? And why?

Ranger Damon let out a muffled groan, part of his mouth buried in the grass. Shane wanted to help him, but was now nervously looking around to see if whoever had attacked him was still nearby. He turned back to Ranger Damon and lifted his foot to take a step when he heard the familiar yowl. He froze, his foot still lifted off of the ground.

Inside the house, through the glass and at a distance, the sound had terrified him. Being out in the woods with nothing to muffle the sound, which had come from disturbingly nearby, Shane was using all of his energy not to piss himself, scream, or vomit. He could hear something moving swiftly through the trees directly behind him, but he couldn't move; he was literally frozen with fear.

He felt the rush of air before he saw the creature leap out of the trees from behind him onto Ranger Damon. Everything seemed to happen fast and yet in slow motion. Shane's knees gave out, and he fell to the ground, staring wide-eyed. The thing let out another yowl as it crouched over Ranger Damon before grabbing him and dragging him into the trees, letting out another yowl, but this time it was a cry of triumph.

Shane's brain took a moment to process the monster that he had just seen. It was a fearsome, humanoid creature with long arms and legs; it had run on all fours but used its front appendages like hands when it had grabbed Ranger Damon. Its skin was pale, with a tinge of blue visible in the beam of the flashlight, and its eyes were large and black, save for a small, glowing dot of light in each that must have been the pupil. Its mouth had been the worst part, large and full of sharp fangs, set underneath a rotten, skeletal nose.

Shane stared at the spot where the thing had disappeared with Ranger Damon. He was stunned, unable to move or make a sound. It had leapt right past him; had it chosen to leap on him, the flashlight would've been useless. All the nights he'd laid in his room, conjuring up images in his mind of what the creature he was hearing would look like, he had never pictured an actual monster like the one he'd just seen.

He finally regained control of his body and scrambled to his feet, running down the path that led back to the cabin, praying that the creature wouldn't suddenly decide to take notice of him. The trail seemed to go on forever, longer than he remembered it being. He thought of Hoodoo Joe saying that he'd seen Greg running, "*like the Devil himself were chasin' him.*" Right when he was thinking that he had taken a wrong turn in his disoriented haste, he broke free of the trees onto his lawn and could see the cabin overlooking the lake, a steadfast sanctuary.

By the time Shane had slipped in the backdoor and locked it behind him, he was gulping in large breaths of air, his hair matted with sweat and his hands shaking. He stumbled into the kitchen, no longer caring if he made noise or woke his parents as he clamored to the dining room, dropping the flashlight on the table and gripping a chair for support while he caught his breath.

He felt like he was going to vomit, pass out, or both. His head was spinning, and he was having trouble staying standing. He was sure that he was going into shock. He closed his eyes and focused on regulating his breathing and preventing vomit from working its way up his throat. His heart rate slowly began to even out, and he opened his eyes, his head a little more level as he released the chair and continued to the wall phone in the kitchen. He grabbed the phone off of the wall and quickly dialed the number for the ranger station. It rang… and rang… and rang.

"Come on, pick up damn it!" Shane growled, slightly bent over; he was so tense that standing up straight seemed like an impossible feat. He slammed the phone into its cradle and dialed again. No one picked up; probably because he'd just seen Ranger Damon dragged into the woods by some kind of creature. But it was Ranger Elton who typically worked the night shift.

He hung the phone up and then started to remove it again. He almost started to dial 911, but then stopped. He considered how it would sound: some kid calling in the middle of the night swearing that he'd just seen someone dragged off by some kind of humanoid creature. They would likely think it was a prank caller. His state of hysteria subsided, replaced by the same dread he'd felt every time he'd heard the creature calling out in the night. No one had believed him when he'd said that he heard the cries; they would be even less likely to if he told them that he had seen a monster.

He placed the phone back in the cradle, feeling defeated. He felt like he was somehow abandoning Ranger Damon by not making the call, but also didn't see how making it would help him if they didn't believe him. He slowly walked back into the dining room, collapsing into one of the chairs.

Hours ticked by, and he finally picked up the flashlight and made himself go upstairs and back to his room. He had to at least try to get some sleep, but he wasn't sure that he would be able to; every time he closed his eyes, he saw the face of that thing right before it had dragged Ranger Damon away into the woods, its pale face and glowing eyes burned into his memory.

Chapter 9

"I saw something in the woods last night," were the first words out of Shane's mouth when he came down for breakfast.

"You went out in the woods last night?" Don asked from behind his paper.

"Yeah," Shane faltered. Maybe telling his parents he'd gone monster hunting was not the best approach. "I couldn't sleep, so I took the flashlight and went for a walk. But I saw something attack and drag off Ranger Damon."

Beth looked concerned, but Don lowered his paper slightly and shook his head. "Shane, you were really worked up yesterday about that nature photographer. You probably just had a nightmare."

"It was not a nightmare; it was real!" Shane insisted, annoyed at his parents' nonchalance about what he'd told them. "Ranger Damon was attacked by an animal last night, and I saw it."

"I'm sure you think that you did. Some nightmares can be very vivid," Don returned to his paper.

Beth decided to interject, "I had some nightmares that I was positive were real when you were younger."

"Haven't either of you heard it? Not even last night when it was so damn close to the cabin!?" Shane blurted in desperation.

His mother set her mouth in a tight frown; he knew that she wanted to scold him for his foul language. Instead, she replied tersely, "Heard what?"

"That awful, screeching yowl," Shane stated adamantly.

"I thought you said that was just the vultures," Don had put down his paper again and was looking at Shane skeptically.

"What's he talking about?" Beth asked, completely lost.

"At first, I thought it was. But I was wrong. It's that thing out there; the thing that got Ranger Damon."

His parents shared a look and then turned back to Shane. "Shane, I can talk to the rangers about getting a signal booster. Maybe being able to talk to your friends more readily would help you feel better. I think you're just bored and looking for excitement where there is none. It was just a bad dream."

Shane shook his head, relinquishing in defeat. "It wasn't…" he said quietly, giving up.

~

Shane stood at the head of the trail. His stomach was in knots; every part of him didn't want to go back into the forest. But a piece of him knew that he had to. He had to try and find some trace of Ranger Damon. He sucked in a deep breath, held it, and then let it out in increments. He took the first step onto the trail.

He'd made the decision to go without Kelsey; he was going to go to the end of the trail where he had found Greg's camera and met Hoodoo Joe, and if he reached the end and had still not found anything, then he would go on his first solo off-trail excursion. He had his map on him, and that one section that he had not explored seemed to draw attention to itself, and for some reason, that bothered him. Probably because he had not seen anything remotely like the piles in Greg's photos, and that was the only place he hadn't explored on the Lake Vautour grounds.

As he came to the section of trail where he had met Hoodoo Joe, he crouched down and was careful to walk quietly. While he was no longer super scared of the hermit, he did not want to be stopped today. Then again, someone had knocked out Ranger Damon and left him in the woods. He knew they said Hoodoo Joe was harmless, but he had thrown large rocks at him. Not the worst crime, but it could do some serious damage – especially if it hit him on the head.

Once he was sure that he was past the camp, he stood up and quickened his pace. He did not want to spend any more time in the woods than he had to. He hiked for what must have been another twenty-five minutes, and then the trail dead ended. He looked both ways, deciding which way to delve in off the trail. He pulled out his map, and it looked like there was more wooded area to the right of the trail than to the left. That would give him more ground to cover, as well as more chance to get lost. But the carcasses – if that was what they were – would have to be farther out, or else he would be able to smell them.

He folded the map and slid it into his pocket. He started off the trail to the right, watching for poison ivy, but seeing none. That was another weird thing; Ranger Elton had warned them about the poison ivy outbreak when they'd arrived. But Shane had gone through his field guides to brush up on what poison ivy looked like so that he would know what to watch for. On his hikes – both alone and with Kelsey – he'd barely seen any poison ivy.

He heard the cawing of birds and flapping of wings somewhere in the distance. Vultures: that was an interesting sign. Next came the smell. Shane actually gagged; it was so pungent. He cupped his hand over his mouth and nose as he followed the sound of the vultures. Nestled in a copse of trees was a small clearing.

He recognized the piles immediately; they were the same ones from the photos on Greg's camera. Despite knowing what to expect, Shane had to turn away, bending over and vomiting his breakfast into the grass. He coughed, wiping his mouth with the back of his hand and turning to look back at the awful scene.

Several vultures were perched on various parts of the mounds, picking at what meat was left on the bones. Shane forced himself to stand up and take a few steps toward them, causing the birds to fly up into the trees in a frenzy, flapping and cawing irritably at having their meal interrupted. Shane looked up at them as he neared the carcasses. It was unsettling how they all stared down at him, watching his every move with their beady eyes set in their pink, wrinkled heads.

Flies buzzed around the piles, not nearly as disturbed by Shane's presence as the vultures. Shane couldn't make out what any one carcass were the remains of; all of the bones had been spread about as they had been eaten on and decayed. Shane could make out what he thought were deer and either coyote or fox skulls. However, some of the bones looked like human bones; Shane had taken anatomy his junior year, and he thought he could pick out a femur, ulna, and part of a pelvis. The more he looked, more humanesque bones seemed to jump out at him, but he tried to tell himself that was impossible. They were animal bones; they just looked similar to human ones.

Something near the top of one of the piles glinted in the light from the sun leaking through the trees, catching Shane's attention. He tried to swallow the lump in his throat as he realized that he'd have to touch some of the remains to see what it was.

He took a deep breath and held it, partially climbing the taller of the piles and reaching for the glinting object. The bones were damp with both morning dew and gore, and Shane tried his best to make sure that he didn't get any liquid on his clothes. His hand finally found the object; it had a different feel than the bones: it was cold and sticky.

He made sure that he had a good grip on it and jumped backward off of the pile. He let out the breath he had been holding and gulped in fresh air – or at least as fresh as it could be surrounded by carcasses. He looked at the object in his hand and almost dropped it, his eyes bulging. It was a gold, blood-smeared, shield-shaped badge with the words 'Lake Vautour Ranger' emblazoned across its surface. The blood was tacky, as if it had been there awhile but not had time to fully dry.

The image of the creature dragging Ranger Damon off the previous night flashed in Shane's mind. He did not want to think it, but the badge was probably his. Which meant that he was probably injured or dead… possibly even in the pile before him. The thought that he may have touched Ranger Damon's remains caused Shane to retch again, but he suppressed throwing up. He refused to entertain that possibility.

He looked around to make sure that no one was watching him, and then begrudgingly slid the badge into his shorts pocket; he would be sure to thoroughly wash out the inside of his pocket before putting them in with the rest of the laundry. He felt like he should hold on to it, just like Greg's camera, but he decided that he would not show it to anyone – at least, not for now. His parents didn't believe him about the creature, and he wasn't sure if anyone else would be inclined to. Either way, it would look bad to be in possession of the bloody badge.

He looked up at the vultures above him. They were all still staring down at him, probably thinking that they wished he would leave so that they could resume their meal. He would oblige them soon; he'd had enough of the disgusting smell and sight. Greg had been right; for them to be roosting at Lake Vautour, they would have to have an ample source of food.

He started toward the trail, but then stopped and looked back at the piles. He could not imagine the creature he had seen stacking its kills in a consistent, out of the way place. Some*one* had stacked them like that… But who? And for what purpose?

He continued toward the trail and heard the flapping of wings as the vultures descended. Ranger Elton had said that the vultures had roosted there for centuries… Had someone always been stacking the bodies, or had the vultures just fed on them scattered, like the deer that had been out on the lawn the morning Ranger Damon had responded to his disturbance call? Only now did it occur to him to wonder how the deer had ended up dead in the first place. It wasn't like it had been hit by a car on their lawn overlooking the lake. The sounds had seemed to be very close that night; that was why he'd called.

He was careful to not get caught by Hoodoo Joe again as he passed by where his camp had been; he definitely did not want to get caught now with the stink of death clinging to him and a missing – presumed dead – ranger's bloody badge in his pocket.

~

Shane had heard the alternative rock music across the lake, so he knew that Rosco was outside working on the boat. He'd hidden the badge in a Ziploc bag in one of his desk drawers and then changed clothes, scrubbing the blood out of the inside of his pocket and throwing his clothes in the wash; he didn't want his parents questioning the smell. Once he put the clothes in the dryer, he hung Greg's camera strap around his neck and started the walk to the Ewan house.

He was glad that by the time he was walking up the drive that he could still hear the music, accompanied by the intermittent sound of power tools. He had originally avoided bringing up the sounds to Rosco because he didn't want him to think that he was a loser, but now he thought that he may be one of the only people who might listen to him.

Shane walked along the dock and saw the stereo sitting in its normal place on the wooden bench, but this time it was not joined by a bottle of beer. He turned his attention to the boat and saw Rosco lying on his stomach, the top half of his body buried in an open floor panel. A beer sat to the side of the open panel, along with an open toolbox and several scattered tools he'd likely been using at one time or another.

"Hey... dude," Shane said loud enough to be heard, then grimaced; he didn't know what had possessed him to add 'dude' on the end of that greeting, but it had sounded stupid.

Rosco placed his hands on each side of the panel and pushed up, his head and shoulders becoming visible as he turned to see who was standing on the dock. "Oh. Hi, Shane," he grinned slightly, his face smeared with black grease. He grunted as he pushed himself the rest of the way up and wiped his hands on his pants. "Almost got it running," he looked proudly at the boat and then back at Shane, running his hand through his hair to get it out of his face. "Kelsey isn't here; I'm not sure where she is."

"Actually, I wanted to talk to you," Shane said nervously, fiddling with the camera.

Rosco noted the seriousness of his tone and looked at him thoughtfully. "What do you wanna talk about?" He noticed the camera hanging around Shane's neck. "That yours?" he pointed at it.

Shane bit his lower lip, shifting the camera to best hide the bloody, cracked lens. "Did you ever see the nature photographer that was here to study the vultures – Greg Sanford?"

Rosco shook his head, "No, but Kelsey told me about him."

"He's missing. I found this camera in the woods. I think it's his." Shane looked at Rosco seriously. "I, uh, think something may have happened to him. Some of the pictures on it are kinda disturbing; they look like piled up bodies- er, mostly animal carcasses."

Rosco crossed his arms, "The blurry ones?" Shane nodded. "Kelsey told me about those too. Who is to say what they are?"

"Would you just look at them?" Shane practically pleaded. "Look at the lens! It's cracked, and I'm pretty sure that's blood." He lifted the camera strap over his head and handed it to Rosco.

Rosco took it and scrutinized the lens. After a moment, he shrugged, "I guess it could be blood. Not enough on it to say." He flipped the camera around and clicked to power it on. After a moment he looked up at Shane cynically. "Battery's dead."

"Fuck," Shane muttered under his breath; he didn't have a charger. He reluctantly took the camera back. "Can I ask you something else?"

"Sure," Rosco picked up his beer and took a swig, leaning on the railing of the boat.

"Have you ever heard or seen anything strange in the woods at night?"

Rosco took a moment before answering. "I can't say that I've ever seen anything; I don't make a habit of going out in the woods at night. But sure, I've heard all kinds of strange things. The wilderness at night produces a lot of strange noises, and the sound carries."

Shane shook his head incredulously, "Doesn't it bother you?"

"Not really," Rosco replied earnestly. "But I guess that's just because I grew up around it." He studied Shane, furrowing his brows. "Have you been hearing things? Did you see something?"

"I thought I did," Shane said quietly. This conversation was becoming all too familiar. "Last night in the woods, I went out to see if I could figure out what kind of animal was making the awful sounds I've been hearing. And I saw some kind of… creature." He debated if he should tell him about Ranger Damon. "… It attacked Ranger Damon."

Rosco stared back at him, a look of concern growing in his eyes. "Attacked…? What did it look like?"

Shane opened his mouth to describe it, but his voice caught in his throat. He knew that Rosco was already skeptical of his story. If he were to describe what he had actually seen, he knew that would be the end of it. "It was too fast for me to get a good look... but it didn't move like something normal. There was just something off about it."

Rosco looked out over the lake, thinking. He turned back to look at Shane seriously, "Look, don't take this the wrong way, but are you sure that you weren't dreaming?" Shane nodded solemnly. "Does Elton know about this?"

"Well, no, I haven't told him. When I called the ranger station last night, no one picked up."

Rosco nodded slowly. Shane could sense how tense Rosco had become at the mention of Ranger Damon. Rosco ran his hand through his hair, noticing how Shane was looking at him. "Look, Damon is nice enough; I just don't like him hanging around here and flirting with my sister. She's just a kid. And he isn't half the ranger Elton is."

He lowered himself back to a laying position on the deck. He looked up at Shane. "Honestly, it was probably just a bad dream. The night sounds have a way of messing with your head; I know. I've had some super weird dreams that I swore were real. But if you really don't feel right about it, go report it to Elton. He may even be able to help you identify what you've been hearing."

"Okay," Shane nodded, forcing a smile and hoping that his tone did not betray how discouraged he felt. He thought back to that feeling of unease he'd had when Ranger Elton had asked about Greg's camera, and he'd lied and said it was his.

"You going to need a ride back?" Rosco asked from inside the engine compartment.

"No thanks," Shane replied, already walking back up the dock. "I could use the exercise."

Chapter 10

Shane stood in the kitchen, staring at the phone. He was working up the courage to call the ranger station. Every interaction that he'd had with Ranger Elton had been uncomfortable, and he was sure that this would be no exception, especially given the subject matter. Shane finally removed the phone from its cradle and dialed the number.

It rang twice before someone picked up, "Lake Vautour ranger station, this is Ranger Elton speaking."

"Hi, this is Shane – Shane Lucas. I'm staying with my parents at–"

"I know who you are. Look, kid, Ranger Damon didn't show up for work this morning. I've really got my hands full here, so unless it is really importa–"

"It is," Shane said seriously and there was silence over the line for a moment.

"What's this about?" he finally said.

"Last night, in the woods, I saw Ranger Damon get attacked by some kind of creature."

There was another long silence over the line. "Where?"

"Near the canoe launch. I could show you."

"Let me wrap up what I'm doing here, and then I'll head out. What kind of animal?"

Shane froze up. "It, uh, moved too fast for me to get a good look."

"All right," Ranger Elton replied, obviously disappointed. "I'll head out there first chance I get. Don't wander off."

Ranger Elton arrived at the cabin roughly an hour after they'd ended their call. Shane had heard his truck coming up the driveway and stepped outside to meet him. Ranger Elton rolled the truck to a stop and climbed out, looking seriously at Shane as he approached.

"Near the canoe launch you said?" he grunted, resting his hands on his hips.

"Yeah," Shane nodded, and the two started down the trail in silence.

As they entered the trees, Ranger Elton spoke without turning to look at Shane, his eyes never leaving the trail, "What were you doing out in the woods last night?"

"Well, um…" Shane thought of the best way to answer and decided that it would be best to just go with the truth. "Remember the disturbance call I made to the station a while back?" Ranger Elton nodded, a slight smirk curving at the corner of his mouth. "I've kept hearing those sounds, and they just do not sound like anything that I've heard before… Not the vultures and not a fox, like Ranger Damon seemed to think. So, I wanted to see if I could figure out what it was." Shane watched Ranger Elton's face as he spoke, but his expression was impossible to read. "Do you think that maybe… the sounds I've been hearing could've been the thing that attacked Ranger Damon?"

Ranger Elton shrugged slightly, "Hard to say, since you can't give me any kind of description. Describe these sounds you say that you've been hearing."

Shane thought back to when the thing had been straddling Ranger Damon's unconscious body, how hearing the howl so close had seemed to rattle not only his eardrums, but all of his insides. He shuddered, "It's a screeching yowl... Almost like a human cry of pain, but twisted and primal, somehow."

Ranger Elton continued walking. "You could've heard anything, or even a combination of things. Sound travels at night out here."

"But what about what I saw?" Shane could feel himself beginning to grow flustered as they reached the break in the trees for the canoe launch.

"I don't really know what to tell you since *you* do not even seem to know what you saw," Ranger Elton looked at Shane for the first time as they came to a stop in the clearing. "You said you saw him here?"

"Yeah," Shane gritted his teeth, trying to keep his tone steady. "He looked like someone had knocked him out... He had a head wound and was just laying there. As I approached him, this... *thing* jumped out of the trees and dragged him off."

Ranger Elton frowned, watching as Shane pointed out where Ranger Damon had been, where he'd been standing, and from where the creature had come and the direction it had run off with Ranger Damon.

He crossed his arms over his chest, "So it was big, then? If it dragged him off, as you say."

"Yeah, big enough. Roughly human-sized."

Ranger Elton harrumphed. "That can't be right; we don't have any wildlife that size 'round these parts."

"But it was! It was big and pale blue."

"Oh, pale blue? You suddenly are remembering a lot of details about

something you could tell me literally
nothing about over the phone," Ranger
Elton retorted mockingly.

"Look, I know what I saw!"

"Do you? So you want me to believe
you saw, what, a Goddamn cryptid?"

"Maybe!" Shane shot back, finally
losing his cool. "I should've known better
than to bother reporting what I saw, even if
Rosco did think that was the right thing to
do!"

"Rosco knows about this?" Ranger
Elton asked in a less degrading tone.

"Yeah... I told him earlier today."

Ranger Elton stared hard at Shane for a
moment and then turned back to the trail
the way that they'd come. "Just forget
about it. You probably just heard or saw
something in the dark and got spooked. I'm
sure that Ranger Damon just overslept or
something is all." He paused and looked
back over his shoulder at Shane, who
hadn't budged. "Well, come on. And
another thing: don't go out hiking at night

again. It isn't safe, especially if you do not know the woods well."

"I know them well enough," Shane huffed, dragging his feet to join Ranger Elton as he resumed his walking.

Ranger Elton harrumphed again, "Kelsey's got you convinced she knows everything there is to know about these woods, I'm sure. You watch yourself, Mr. Lucas. And do *not* go off the trail unless you want to get a nasty case of poison ivy."

"I haven't seen any," Shane muttered, and Ranger Elton shot him a look out of the corner of his eye. "Hey," he said louder. "Do you know what happened to Greg Sanford, the nature photographer? I haven't seen him since he was setting up that first day, and all of his equipment is gone."

"He left – went home. Nothing to see," Ranger Elton replied confidently.

"Doesn't that strike you as a little… odd? I mean, the guy seemed totally obsessed with the vultures."

"So long as he's out of my hair, who cares why he left? I'm glad he's gone; one less thing for me to worry about, especially with Ranger Damon MIA." They had reached the Lucases' cabin. Ranger Elton walked to his truck and opened the driver door, then turned to face Shane before getting in. He stroked his beard, "I'll make a note of what you reported, but I'm sure that Ranger Damon will turn up. Stay safe out there."

Shane didn't answer, just watched him climb in his truck and drive away. A piece of him felt like he should've shown him the bloody Lake Vautour ranger badge up in his room. The other part of him felt like it was still best to keep that to himself, especially since he didn't know who had knocked out Ranger Damon and left him out in the woods in the first place. It was almost as if he'd been left out for the creature; why else would he have been left out in the open instead of hidden in the foliage if whoever it was just wanted to leave him for dead?

~

Shane watched the sun rise over Lake Vautour as he cast the fishing line into the water. He didn't have a fishing permit, but figured that no one would really catch him. He'd never been one for fishing, but had decided to get out his dad's fishing pole and tackle box to see if he'd acquired a liking for it; after all, he hadn't been fishing since he was nine or ten. Plus, it was something different to do.

He was still sour about Ranger Elton's reception of his report about the animal sighting and Ranger Damon, and did not feel much like hiking. The little red and white bobber floated on the surface of the water – nothing was biting. Fishing was still just as boring as he remembered, but it gave him a chance to be doing something while doing nothing. And some time to think.

He heard someone coming and very quickly reeled in the line. If it was Ranger Elton, he knew that he'd want any excuse to bust his balls for fishing without a permit. He just seemed like that sort.

Kelsey emerged from the brush. "Rosco said you came by yesterday," she said, approaching him. She spotted the fishing pole in his hands and the tackle box in the grass by his feet. "You fish?"

"Uh, no, not really. Just giving my dad's pole a try," he laughed nervously; he had let himself get worked up over nothing. "And yeah, I did come by yesterday. He said he almost has the boat up and running."

"Mm-hm," Kelsey nodded, examining her nails. "What did you two talk about?"

"Probably nothing you'd be interested in."

"Guy stuff?"

"No," Shane smirked. "I just don't think that you'd be interested is all."

Kelsey smiled devilishly and rolled her eyes, crossing her arms, "Still hung up on Greg Sanford?"

Shane looked at her coldly, "Not really. But that, right there, is exactly why I do not even think you'd be interested." Shane removed the bobber from the end of the fishing line and wiped it on the grass before replacing it in the tackle box. "Seen Ranger Damon the past couple of days?"

Kelsey sighed heavily, "Is that why you're acting like a jerk? You think I've been out with Damon?"

Shane scowled, "No, it was an honest question. I have a reason for asking; just humor me."

Kelsey shook her head and rolled her eyes, "No, I haven't seen him in a few days."

Shane took a deep breath before continuing, "A couple nights ago, I was out in the woods, and I saw him get attacked by some kind of… I don't know what it was. But I think it might have killed him, and no one believes me. Ranger Elton is sure he just overslept or had some other reason for not showing up to work, but I know that's not the case."

Kelsey looked at him, concerned. She walked over next to him and rested her hand on his shoulder. "What kind of... 'thing?'"

Shane looked deep into her eyes. He wanted to tell her the truth; he wanted to feel like he could tell someone and not have them tell him that he'd dreamed or imagined it. Of all the people on the lake, he *wanted* Kelsey to believe him the most.

"If I tell you the truth, will you believe me?"

"I'll do my best," she replied, no longer smirking.

Shane took a deep breath and lowered himself to the grass, sitting cross legged. Kelsey did the same. "I'd gone out in the woods to see if I could figure out what'd been making that awful yowling. I thought that if I could figure out what it was, that it would put my mind at ease – that it wouldn't bother me anymore." He closed his eyes, the memory playing over in his mind and causing his heart to start pounding; he could feel beads of sweat forming on his brow even in the cool morning.

"I came across Ranger Damon in the woods, and then I heard the yowling nearby. And this *thing* leapt out of the trees onto him. It was like nothing I've ever seen before, Kelsey. It dragged him off into the woods, and I'm not proud to say that I just ran back here and locked myself inside."

"What did it look like?" Kelsey asked, playing with a few blades of grass.

"It was, um… kind of like a person. I guess 'humanoid' would be the word. It had a bald head that pretty much looked like a skull, with the nose rotted away and the eyes large and dark. The mouth was horrible and lined with fangs instead of teeth. Its limbs were so long that they looked disproportionate to its body, yet

somehow it managed to move super fast."
Shane shook his head, feeling sick. "I've
never seen anything like it, even in horror
movies. It was kind of... blue, which was
also weird. And when it let out that awful
sound right next to me like that... It felt
like it rattled everything inside of me down
to my core. Just thinking about it makes
my ears ring."

He looked up at Kelsey to read her
expression, but she was just staring blankly
at the grass she'd been playing with. After
a moment, she looked up at Shane. She
took in air to speak, but then just sat in
silence.

"Well...?" Shane finally asked to break
the silence.

"That is a lot to ask me to believe," she
finally said.

Shane's shoulders slumped. "I know
what I saw; you said you would believe
me!"

"I said I'd do my best, but Shane, this
is too much. I'm sure you saw something,

but… What you described, it just doesn't make sense. And what was Damon doing out in the woods anyway? Night shift stays in the station unless they get called out to check on something."

"Maybe he was checking on something." Shane didn't want to get into the fact that he'd found Ranger Damon bludgeoned and unconscious; that had not done anything to help his case with Ranger Elton.

"Shane," Kelsey reached over and rested her hand on his. "I know that whatever you have been hearing has been bothering you. But there has to be some other explanation for it, right? And maybe Elton was right – maybe Damon does have a reason for not coming into work."

"Yeah – he's dead!" Shane shouted, angrily pulling his hand out of Kelsey's grasp and standing there glaring at her.

"Shane, calm down," she begged, taken aback by his outburst.

"Calm down!? How am I supposed to calm down? I saw Ranger Damon get dragged off by some kind of monster, and no one seems to give a shit!" He snatched up his father's fishing pole and tackle box, storming back up to the cabin.

"Shane, wait–" Kelsey called after him, getting up onto her knees. He kept going and went inside, slamming the door behind him. He was glad that he didn't wake his parents; he didn't want to have to explain to them why he was slamming the door, but also, to some extent, he didn't care. They slept through everything out here, anyway.

Chapter 11

Shane had waited by one of the back windows for Kelsey to leave, watching her through the curtains. It hadn't taken her long; she'd watched the house for a few minutes, waiting to see if he would get over his fit and come back. She had finally stood, starting for home and casting one final glance over her shoulder. She had likely decided it was best to leave him be for the time being, and that was the right call.

Once he was sure that she was gone, Shane had immediately set out for Hoodoo Joe's camp. He hadn't wanted her to try and talk him down, or even worse, try to follow him and talk him out of what he was doing. Hoodoo Joe was the only person who had taken his other claims and concerns seriously; if anyone would believe him about what he'd seen, it would be him. He might even know what exactly Shane had seen, be able to offer some explanation.

Shane reached the point in the path where he was sure that Hoodoo Joe had thrown the rocks at him. He looked around to get his bearings and walked in the direction that he was almost positive that he remembered the camp being. He stopped dead in his tracks as he reached the spot. There was no tent. He could make out where Hoodoo Joe had had his fire burning, although it would appear that he had taken great pains to cover the area with leaves and branches. The log with the worn spots from being frequently sat on also remained, so he knew he had the right spot.

Shane looked around him, spinning in circles and looking for some sign of the old hermit. "Hoodoo Joe!" he called out, cupping his hands around his mouth. There was no answer aside from the cawing of birds in the distance, likely crows or maybe a few stray vultures. "Hoodoo Joe!" he hollered again, walking farther into the clearing.

Shane felt an overwhelming sense of isolation and hopelessness begin to envelop him. Hoodoo Joe could be anywhere; Kelsey had told him that he moved his camp often, that even in all of her exploring, she'd never actually found it. He also remembered Hoodoo Joe telling him that he'd seen Shane hiking with Kelsey, and neither of them had even known that he was there. He could be watching Shane right now and just choosing to stay hidden.

"Hoodoo Joe!" Shane cried out desperately, fighting back a sob. He stood in the clearing a moment longer before admitting defeat to himself and starting back toward the trail. Hoodoo Joe had obviously moved his camp – if he was even still alive.

A chill ran down Shane's spine as he thought about the creature that had gotten Ranger Damon. With just the tent as shelter, Hoodoo Joe would be an easy target. But he had also lived in these woods for years and never been harmed by the thing. And there was still the possibility that he was the one responsible for bludgeoning Ranger Damon. Maybe he knew that Shane had found Ranger Damon and finally run for the hills, but for some reason, that seemed unlikely to Shane.

"Hoodoo Joe!" he yelled as he made his way back down the trail. It was a long shot, but maybe he was somewhere nearby where he would be able to hear him.

Shane continued to call out his name every so often, but by the time he emerged onto the cabin's lawn, he had neither heard nor seen any sign of the elusive hermit. Shane hung his head dejectedly as he tromped up to the back door.

Before going inside, he turned and looked out over the lake. He knew one thing: There was no way that he was going back out into those woods at night again. At least not without a hunting rifle, which were banned on Lake Vautour, and he didn't have one anyway.

~

A few more days had gone by without any sign of Ranger Damon. Shane knew this from wandering near the ranger station and only seeing Ranger Elton coming and going, usually cussing under his breath about something or just scowling. He had also called the ranger station a few times, just to see who would pick up. When Ranger Elton's gruff voice had droned, "Lake Vautour ranger station," through the receiver, Shane had quickly hung up every time.

He had also not seen any sign of Hoodoo Joe during that time. He had hiked various paths and ventured into some of the territories he had mapped out with Kelsey, but had not seen any signs of the camp or the hermit himself.

One thing he'd noticed that had definitely not been there before were carvings on some of the trees. They were scattered in a seemingly random way on various trees along several of the trails. They all looked the same: two feathered arrows pointing inwardly at a solid circle. Shane wondered who had put them there or what they could mean, but hadn't had decent enough Wi-Fi to Google anything about the symbol. For the time being, he decided to shrug them off; maybe it was someone's way of marking the trail. Or some kind of hoodoo symbol.

He'd been sitting outside at the picnic table by the fire ring, studying his map and doodling the carved symbol on the corner, when Kelsey had come walking up the hill to join him. They had not spoken since his outburst when she hadn't believed him about the monster, just like everyone else.

"Hey," she said sheepishly, looking at her feet and kicking at the grass. Shane considered saying, "Hey," back, but decided to stick with the silent treatment. A few seconds passed, and Kelsey continued, "Shane, I'm sorry for not hearing you out the other day." Shane stopped his doodling and looked up at her, genuinely surprised. "It all just seems really farfetched, but there is the fact that Damon seems to be missing."

Shane's shoulders slumped at the mention of Ranger Damon; while he did not wish him dead, there was something about hearing Kelsey say his name that made his blood boil. She seemed to notice his agitation and sat down across from him, gripping his hand and smiling sweetly at him.

She seemed to be looking for the right words. "Weird things have always happened around the lake... I just never thought much of it because that was *normal* to me. It was just the way things always had been."

Shane looked up at her. "What do you mean 'weird things'?"

She half shrugged, shaking her head. "I don't know... Like there were certain years it seemed like there was less wildlife, and people would report livestock and pets missing. Some people just… vanish; but that happens everywhere, right? We're hardly special in that regard. And then there are weird sounds at night sometimes… but you just kinda get used to it." She looked past Shane's shoulder toward the woods. "And those damn birds… They've supposedly always been here, but they're just–" she rolled her eyes, "creepy. I mean, shit, they only really eat dead things. But I really have never seen anything like what you described in the woods. It kinda freaks me out, like, if that's real… it lives right in my backyard…"

Her voice trailed off, and she looked out over the lake, tears glimmering in her eyes. She quickly wiped them away with her free hand, squeezing Shane's hand with the other. "But yeah, basically I came over here to say that I'm sorry for not believing you… I kinda hope you're wrong about what you saw, because–" she shuddered. "But I'm going to try to be open-minded.

Maybe if we figure out what's out there, we can figure out what happened to Damon."

"And Greg Sanford," Shane interjected, and Kelsey fought the urge to roll her eyes. He turned his map around so that it was right-side up for Kelsey and slid it across the table. "Do you know what this symbol means?" he asked, pointing at the two arrows and the dot.

Kelsey studied it for a moment, frowning pensively. She looked up at Shane, "Where'd you see it?"

"In the woods. It's been carved into several trees along the trails, and the carvings look fresh. Someone is putting them there… but why?"

Kelsey shrugged, "Beats me. Maybe it's just some kid pulling a prank."

"So you or me?" Shane chuckled. "You said it yourself; we're the only teenagers here. And what kind of prank would it be, anyway?"

"Something to get up Elton's craw," Kelsey smirked, giggling a little. She grew serious again, "Honestly, I have no idea; I've never seen that before – along the trails or otherwise."

Shane stroked his chin, exhaling out his nostrils – another dead end. He turned the map back to him and studied the symbol closer.

"Does that say 'Hoodoo Joe's camp'?" Kelsey asked, pointing at a spot on the map.

Shane's eyes bulged as he felt his ears grow hot. "Um, yeah, I thought it might be there, but it wasn't. See the question mark." He forced a laugh. "I just forgot to erase it." He quickly erased the entry, making sure to leave a shadow of the writing intact for later; he just did not necessarily want Kelsey to go poking around where the campsite had been and possibly getting rocks chucked at her, or worse.

"I told you," she said, shaking her head. "I've *never* found it, and I know these woods like the back of my hand."

"So, you've never found the piles of carcasses either?"

Kelsey set her mouth in a firm line, "No, I haven't. Which is why I keep telling you: those aren't what were in Greg's pictures. They were blurry; they could've been of anything."

A piece of Shane wanted to tell her that he knew better because he'd seen them up close and personal, but he decided to keep that to himself; divulging that information could lead to more uncomfortable topics, like if there were in fact human bones mingled in with the animals and the bloody ranger badge up in his room.

"Yeah," he said dismissively, sliding his hand out of hers to hold the map steady while he refined some lines on the symbol with his pencil. He thought he saw her grit her teeth due to him pulling his hand away, and he fought the urge to smirk.

"So," Kelsey sat up straighter and said in a noticeably more chipper tone, "I have news!" Shane looked up at her and raised his eyebrows, waiting. "Rosco has the boat up and running. He's gonna take it for a test drive tomorrow! If all goes well, we can go out on it soon." She grinned, "I was hoping he'd have it done before you went back home." Shane smiled back. He felt her hand nudge his on the table, and he willingly took it.

~

Shane had spotted the small fire across the lake at dusk, just after dinner. He could tell that it was on the Ewans' back patio in the fire ring that he'd seen. He'd set out to make the twenty-five minute walk to the house; he wanted to smooth things over with Rosco, since he wanted him to *actually* want to hang out with him and not think that he was some kind of weirdo.

He'd walked up the driveway and tried the front door, but when no one answered, he'd walked around the back to the patio. He spotted Rosco, slouched in one of the patio chairs, but Kelsey was nowhere to be seen.

"Hey," Shane said quietly, leaving off the 'dude' this time; it just wasn't his style.

Rosco looked up at him and gave a small nod. "What's up?"

"Saw the fire across the lake and thought I'd join you, if you don't mind. My parents never wanna use our fire ring." Shane chuckled.

"Yeah, sure. Kelsey went to bed early, so the company would be nice. You can even have a beer if you want; just don't tell anyone."

"Yeah, sure, thanks," Shane said eagerly, taking a chair as Rosco popped the top off of a fresh beer and handed it to him. He took a sip; it tasted kind of bitter, but he was stoked just to be invited to sit down and have a beer with Rosco. "Kelsey told me you got the boat up and running."

"Yeah. It was a son of a bitch, but finally got it," Rosco took a swig of his beer. "Going to take it for a spin on the water tomorrow if the weather holds up, just to make sure everything's running right when it's not docked."

"Yeah, totally." Shane took another drink of his beer.

"It felt good to be working on an engine again. That's what I went to trade school for, and I was going to open a garage," Rosco said reminiscently, looking out over the dock and the lake.

A tense silence hung between the two of them. Shane glanced over at Rosco out of the corner of his eye and saw him still just staring out over the lake. "Do you mind if I ask what happened to you and Kelsey's parents?" Shane asked awkwardly; he didn't know what had compelled him to ask; maybe it was Rosco's mention of what might have been. "If you don't wanna talk about it, I completely understand."

Rosco let out a sigh, and Shane glanced at him again to see that he'd dropped his gaze down to his beer. "It's only natural to be curious," he said, but his voice had taken on a morose thickness. "It's probably better that you ask me instead of Kelsey, especially if she hasn't mentioned it to you." Shane shook his head. Rosco looked back out over the water, "It happened a little over three years ago. They'd gone out for dinner and drinks that night, so they decided to drive into town. It was late when they headed back, so the fog had set in from the lake…" His voice trailed off, and he fiddled with his beer bottle. "Something must have happened that made them lose control of the car; that was all anyone could figure.

"They both died instantly, or at least that's what the coroner said." He took a deep breath, "I, uh, never saw the bodies. Elton assured me that they were in such a state that they had to be cremated. I didn't argue; everything was up to me, as dictated in their wills and due to being the next of kin anyway. I was only twenty-three years old, and fresh out of trade school. But I took on guardianship of Kelsey so that we wouldn't be separated. With our parents gone… we were pretty much all the other had."

He looked over at Shane, chuckling, "But being responsible for a fourteen year old is not an easy task, especially when you're only in your early twenties. I put the garage on hold; the life insurance was plenty for the two of us to live on, and I figured I could get some other job until Kelsey graduates and heads off to college."

Shane sat in stunned silence. He tried to imagine if he lost both of his parents in the blink of an eye like that… He would be completely lost. He didn't even have any siblings to turn to; he'd likely be shipped off to live with one set of his grandparents or the other. "I'm sorry for your loss…" Shane said quietly, almost regretting that he'd asked.

Rosco polished off the rest of his beer and nodded sadly. "It is what it is; it happened. Sure, it sucks, but… can't change it." He gripped the armrests of his chair and stood. "Wanna have a look around the boat?"

"Oh yeah, sure," Shane replied, relieved that there didn't seem to be any hard feelings for him breaching the uncomfortable topic.

He got up and followed Rosco out onto the dock. He had never been out on the water at night; there was something peaceful about it, hearing the water gently lapping at the dock posts just beneath their feet and the sides of the boat. Rosco bent over the side and picked up a small, battery powered Coleman lantern from the deck and clicked it on so that they could see.

"Be careful as you step on, since the dock is stationary and the boat is floating," Rosco warned, stepping onto the boat and holding out his arm for if Shane needed to steady himself. Shane felt like he did pretty well for not having been on a boat since he was thirteen and having been drinking.

Rosco started to show him around,
beginning with the bow.

Chapter 12

Shane had borrowed the car to go into town. He'd said that he wanted to check things out and just see the place, since he hadn't left the lake since they'd arrived. While that was half true, his real motive for going into town was to buy a charger for Greg's camera. He had been sure that the town had to have at least one store with a decent electronics section, and he had been right; the associate had been all too happy to help him find one that would be compatible with his camera.

He had walked around a little afterward, but decided to head back; he wanted to charge the camera as soon as possible and try to show his parents the photos; maybe then they would at least believe part of his story. And he could show Rosco.

When he'd gotten back to the cabin, he had gone straight upstairs and plugged the camera in. After that, he'd walked downstairs to find his father and Ranger Elton bent over the modem.

"Damn thing just *never* works, even when the weather's good," he heard his father saying as he walked into the room and sat down on the sofa.

Ranger Elton looked up as he sat down. "Hello, Shane," he grunted. Shane simply nodded back. Ranger Elton turned back to Don, "I can install a signal booster, but that's going to cost you extra."

"Sure, whatever, just get the thing working," Don waved him off.

"It may take me a little while to get back over here since I'm currently manning the station by myself," Ranger Elton said as he stood upright and adjusted his belt.

"What happened to Ranger Damon? Did he take a vacation?" Don asked.

"Pfft, who knows? He's fucked off to somewhere… Hasn't been in to work in two weeks, and I can't seem to get ahold of him."

"That's strange, he seemed very conscientious when we met him," Beth interjected as she entered the room with a tray containing a pitcher of fresh lemonade and glasses. "Here, for your trouble. Oh, Shane, I didn't realize you were back. Do you want me to grab you a glass?"

"Sure, I'll have a little," Shane stood and headed for the stairs. "It'll be refreshing before I go out on another hike." Ranger Elton's face darkened slightly, but it was a passing expression; he sipped his lemonade and thanked Beth.

Once Shane had had his lemonade, he set off into the woods to look for Hoodoo Joe and possibly more clues as to where the creature inhabited; as the days had passed, he had become less apprehensive about going out in the woods during the daytime, since the creature seemed to only be active at night.

He wandered along a trail that he hadn't taken in a while; as a matter of fact, not since his original adventures with

Kelsey. As he walked along the trail, he noticed another one of the strange carvings in one of the trees. Someone had gone to an awful lot of trouble to spread them out and make sure that they were all along the many trails. Shane still wished he had a way of knowing what purpose they served or what they meant.

It had been a couple of hours by the time Shane made it back to the cabin. He walked in to find his father typing away at his laptop. "Internet is *finally* working. That signal booster seems to be exactly what we needed."

Shane nodded and walked into the kitchen where he could hear his mother putting away dishes. She seemed flustered when he entered and managed a small smile when she noticed him. "Hey, honey, how was your walk?"

"Good, Mom," he replied, opening the fridge and pulling out a can of Sprite. He went into the living room and sat down at the table. Once she had finished with the dishes, his mother joined them.

A few minutes passed, and then she broke the silence, "What do you think about what Ranger Elton told us about Ranger Damon? He did not seem like the type to just skip work, at least without calling. I sure hope something didn't happen to him..."

Shane looked up at her and stole a quick glance at his father before saying, "I told you that I saw something attack him the other night."

"Shane, please, not that again," his father sighed, rolling his eyes.

"Well, I did. And I got a charger for that camera I found... I could show you the pictures. Just look at them and tell me if you think there is something weird in them."

"Shane, we told you to give that camera to Ranger Elton," Beth said incredulously.

"Look, please just look at them. Then, I'll give it to Ranger Elton." Shane got up before they could protest and headed up the stairs to his room. He hoped they would believe his lie; at least for the time being, he had no intention of giving the camera over to Ranger Elton. He opened the door to his room and froze in his tracks.

The camera and charger were gone. Shane was positive that he'd left them out, since the camera needed to charge. He stared at the empty space on his desk for a few seconds longer before closing the door and slowly starting back down the steps.

"I can't find it..." he said quietly, then looked up at his parents. "Did Ranger Elton go upstairs?"

"Yeah, he had to run a wire. But I don't think he would've gone in your room, and he definitely wouldn't have taken that camera."

"Yeah, you're right... Guess I just misplaced it," Shane did his best to act nonchalant.

He could think of no other reason for the camera to be missing. Ranger Elton had likely pieced it together that the camera Shane had was Greg's after seeing him that day in the woods, and then how Shane had been so adamant about him being missing when he'd told him about seeing Ranger Damon get attacked.

Shane was sure now that Ranger Elton had lied about losing his camera in the woods and had been looking for Greg's. He obviously wanted to see what was on that camera, which only confirmed Shane's suspicions that Greg was in fact missing, and Ranger Elton was trying to keep it under wraps. But why? Bad publicity? Or something much darker?

Shane turned around and went back upstairs. He might as well make good use of the boosted Internet.

~

Shane stepped outside and breathed in the fresh air. He had checked his messages from his friends back home. That all seemed so distant now, with their sports practice and bowling alleys and matinees. Shane had much bigger things to worry about, like a monster and a potential human killer on the loose. He had replied back to them that everything was fine, the trails were great, Kelsey was great, and that he had made a new older friend who let him drink beer and check out his boat. He figured his promise to Rosco to not tell anyone that he'd let him drink did not apply to 'the guys.'

After that, he had tried to dig up some information about the symbol he'd seen carved into the trees, with no luck. Most of what had come up were various geometry equations or coding references – nothing that referred to what he was seeing, he was sure.

Shane stretched his back and looked out over the lake. He spotted a movement near the shore of the canoe launch and squinted to see better. His eyes instantly widened when he recognized the straw hat: Hoodoo Joe!

"Hey!" he hollered, and Hoodoo Joe's head snapped up, spotting him across the lake. He quickly looked back at what he was doing and seemed to pick up the pace. Shane bounded to the trail; he did not want Hoodoo Joe to disappear into the woods without getting to ask him some much needed questions. He caught him just as he was picking up the last of some crudely made crayfish traps. "Hey," Shane said, out of breath, but standing so that he was blocking Hoodoo Joe's path. He placed his hands on his hips, breathing in large gasps. "Where've you been?"

Hoodoo Joe grinned a knowing, gap-toothed grin. "Around," he answered complacently.

"What does that mean? I've been looking all over for you. I revisited the camp, and it was gone."

Hoodoo Joe shrugged, "I move da camp often. As I said, I've been around."

"If you were around, then why didn't you answer me when I was calling for you?"

Hoodoo Joe shrugged again, "Guess we were on different sides of da forest."

Shane narrowed his eyes. "Sure."

Hoodoo Joe set down his traps, "So… What do you wanna talk about dat is so important, *cher*?"

Shane grew sheepish, "I, uh, saw something… that I can't explain in the woods the other night. About two weeks ago."

Hoodoo Joe looked at him suspiciously, the curves of a smile tugging at the corners of his mouth, "What were you doin' in da woods at night?"

"I wanted to see if I could figure out what was making those sounds I was hearing," Shane answered, almost defensively. "And I saw something attack Ranger Damon… It howled, just like what

I've been hearing. Nobody else believes me, but it looked kinda human. It didn't have any hair and was kind of a whitish blue, with large dark eyes that had a strange glow and a mouth full of fangs. Its limbs were long and gangly, yet it moved super fast. It dragged Ranger Damon off into the woods. I think it may have killed him, may have even been what the nature photographer was running from." He hesitated, "… Have you ever seen anything like that?"

Hoodoo Joe scratched his scraggly beard and chuckled, "And people say dat I'm crazy. No, can't say dat I have." Shane hung his head in disappointment. Hoodoo Joe grew serious and rested his hand on Shane's shoulder. When Shane looked at him, he was staring intensely into Shane's eyes with his mismatched ones, "Do not go lookin' for dem – Ranger Damon or da photographer. Or go out in da woods at night anymore. Lake Vautour is a friendly enough place, but at night, da same cannot be said. I've lived in dese woods long enough to know just how cruel da darkness can be." He released Shane's shoulder and picked up his traps. He started into the trees.

"One more thing," Shane said loudly. Hoodoo Joe paused and looked back over his shoulder. "What does that symbol mean?" Shane pointed at the symbol carved into one of the nearby trees.

Hoodoo Joe looked up at it and then back at Shane, "It's an ancient Native American symbol. It's meant to ward off evil spirits."

"Did you put them there?" Shane asked, but Hoodoo Joe had already turned and was making his way through the trees. "Did you put them there!?" Shane raised his voice, but the hermit simply disappeared among the trees without a word. Shane stared after him a moment longer before turning and walking back along the trail to their cabin.

When he got back, he went straight back up to his room and fired up his laptop. He Googled the Native American symbol for warding off evil spirits. He felt a chill roll down his spine as he clicked the Images tab and the results loaded. While there were various symbols that had come up, the one that was consistent was a dot flanked by two inward facing arrows. It would seem that Hoodoo Joe had told him the truth. But that still didn't answer if he or someone else had put them there.

"Shane!" his mother called up the stairs. "Kelsey's here!"

"I'll be right down!" he called back. He stared at his computer screen for a moment, then closed the lid and headed downstairs, pulling his bedroom door closed behind him.

When he got to the first floor, Kelsey was waiting for him and practically jumping up and down with excitement. "Rosco said the boat is ready to take out! It passed all of his tests. Come on! He even let me bring the car to come get you so we wouldn't have to walk." She waved enthusiastically to Beth as she took Shane by the hand and practically dragged him through the front door. "He *never* lets me take the car," she added callously once they were outside. Shane couldn't help but think back to Rosco's story of what had happened to their parents, but kept that thought to himself.

Shane was quiet the short ride from the cabin to the Ewans' house as Kelsey babbled on excitedly about how it had been over a year since they had gotten to take the boat out. He was still processing the symbol, its meaning, and who had put them there – and if it had anything to do with the creature he'd seen attack Ranger Damon. Kelsey turned into the driveway and followed the curve back around the house where she parked it in the garage.

They exited out the side door, and Shane spotted Rosco on the boat, the low revving of the engine audible from where they stood. He waved, and Shane waved back. He and Kelsey made their way down the dock and climbed carefully onto the boat.

"You two ready to set sail?" Rosco asked, smiling. "There are beers and sodas in the cooler," he pointed and winked.

They set off across the lake, which Shane realized was even larger than it looked when you were out in the open and not near the shore. It seemed to stretch on for miles in every direction, but he was sure that was just an illusion since he could see the Ewans' house from his backyard. Shane looked around at the surrounding shorelines as they went by, noticing several other nice houses like the Ewans', as well as a few other cabins. He couldn't help but wonder if Hoodoo Joe was watching them from the trees...

Once they were near what seemed to be the center of the lake, Rosco stopped the boat and let it glide on its own, grabbing a beer from the cooler and sitting on the edge with his legs dangling over, looking out over the lake.

Shane took this opportunity to bring up the symbol to Kelsey as they sat on the deck together, also sipping beers; Shane was slowly acquiring a taste for the stuff. "So, I ran into Hoodoo Joe earlier today."

"What!? I told you, it's better to just stay away from him!"

Shane shrugged, "He knows a lot about the woods, and he told me what that symbol carved in the trees means; it's a Native American symbol to ward off evil spirits."

"And how do you know he didn't just lie to you?"

"Because we got a signal booster in the cabin, and I looked it up. What he said checks out. Now I just wonder if it was him or someone else who put them there... And if it has to do with the creature."

Kelsey gripped Shane's hand, looking seriously into his eyes, "Don't worry about that right now; we can look more into it later. For now, just enjoy the boat." She leaned into him and kissed him. Shane froze, utterly stunned, and even though it only lasted for a few seconds, he felt like their lips were joined forever. As she pulled away, he sat in dazed silence, and Kelsey giggled, squeezing his hand. "Don't tell Rosco… At least not now," she whispered, kissing his cheek and not surprising him quite so much this time.

Shane could feel his heart beating out of his chest. His first kiss, and he'd fumbled by just freezing up; he hadn't even kissed her back, he'd been caught so off guard. He took another sip of his beer; the bottle felt strange against his lips after the kiss.

"Uh, yeah, sure," he stammered, blushing and smiling at her. They continued to sit on the deck, looking up at the sky and out over the lake, sipping their drinks and holding hands.

~

Shane sat up in his room, trying to focus on digging up information about what the creature could be, but his mind kept wandering back to Kelsey. They had kissed again in the car when she'd dropped him off, and this time he'd been ready for it and done his part.

He was feeling a strange mix of emotions; while the kisses themselves had made him feel elated, now he felt troubled and was filled with questions. What did the kisses mean? Were they just friends who were attracted to each other, or were they going to be something more? And then there was the fact that Shane would have to go home at the end of the summer, which was only a little over a month away.

He turned back to his computer, tapping the keys aimlessly and considering what to search. He knew that finding the information he needed wouldn't be easy; just finding out anything about the symbol carved in the trees had been difficult until Hoodoo Joe had given him some direction.

216

He had tried searching anything from local cryptids to Native American demons, but had not gotten any real results – definitely not anything that came remotely close to what he had witnessed. That meant that he was either not typing in the right keywords or it wasn't something that he was going to find on the Internet.

He closed his laptop and went to the window, looking out. He tried to remember if he'd seen a library while he'd been in town. He didn't think so, but that did not mean that there wasn't one. Maybe he'd drive into town the next day and see if he could find anything. Then again, he could not imagine that there would be any record of such a creature.

He plopped down on his bed and stared at the ceiling. If the symbol on the trees was related to the creature – and he couldn't imagine what else they would be there for – that meant that *someone* believed the creature was evil and was grasping at straws to keep it away. And if that were true, he was inclined to think that his family may not be safe… Rosco and Kelsey may not be safe.

But he also didn't know how he'd be able to convince his parents to leave the lake cabin early, and a piece of him did not want to leave because of Kelsey. He felt a kind of obligation to figure out a way to stop what was out there before it could hurt anyone else, especially his parents, Kelsey, or Rosco. And he still had some burning questions about why Ranger Elton had wanted Greg's camera so badly – badly enough to steal it.

Chapter 13

Kelsey had come over before the sun was even up, which had put Shane on edge for multiple reasons. For one, that meant she was out alone in the night with that *thing* on the loose. Secondly, he did not want her accidently throwing rocks at the wrong window and waking up his parents.

"What are you doing here?" he'd hissed in a loud whisper when he'd finally pulled on some clothes and made his way to the back door.

She shrugged, smiling at him, "I just thought maybe we could watch the sun rise over the lake together. Kinda romantic."

Shane blushed, feeling guilty for being irritated with her. "That actually does sound kinda nice."

The two had laid in the grass on the hill for a while in silence, holding hands and watching the line of orange along the lake grow taller and brighter as the sun rose, lighting up the water. When the sky had taken on an ombre orange to lavender hue, Shane looked over at Kelsey as he decided to try breaching the subject of the creature again, "So, I'm gonna go into town later today to see if I can find any record or lore of a creature like what I saw at the library. I was wondering if you would wanna come with me… I figure you might know where to look for something like that."

Kelsey exhaled heavily through her nostrils, looking over at Shane with a look of incredulous pity, "You won't find anything. Believe me, I know; I read every book in that library growing up."

Shane looked back over the lake and gritted his teeth in disappointment and was surprised to find himself fighting tears. Kelsey reached over and gently gripped his jaw, turning his head to face her again. She looked into his eyes, "We will figure out what's out there. Books and Google just aren't gonna be able to help us."

Shane managed a small smile, "Yeah… You're right. But where do we start?"

"Well…" Kelsey propped herself up on her elbows, sitting up slightly. "You've said you only ever hear this thing at night?" Shane nodded. "And you saw it attack Damon–" she choked on his name, and despite his jealously, Shane felt bad for her; after all, she knew that she'd likely lost a friend, "-at night?" Shane nodded again. "Then that would make it nocturnal. Which means it has to go to its den or whatever during the day." She grinned over at Shane, the stark light of the sunrise illuminating her face with a golden glow, "That means if we find the den during the daytime, it'll be vulnerable."

Shane's smile grew, but then shrunk again, "But that still doesn't answer where we start looking."

"Somewhere not heavily traveled… Maybe near your carcasses?" she suggested, and Shane felt his stomach lurch. He never wanted to go near those macabre edifices again. Kelsey noticed his look of discomfort and giggled good-naturedly. "We don't have to go *right* up to them; just nearby. I'm sure that it's not right by where it puts its leftovers; I can't imagine the vultures would be cool feeding so close to that."

"Good point. Should we start looking today?" Shane suggested.

"Yeah, sure. I mean, we have nothing better to do," Kelsey giggled again, and Shane could already feel some of the tension leaving him. "But if we are gonna do that, I need to go home and get ready. Have some breakfast and be ready in hour," she instructed him, standing and brushing off her shorts.

She started in the direction of her house, then turned and trotted back to Shane, squatting and planting a kiss on his lips. While caught partially off guard, Shane was better prepared this time and returned the gesture.

"See you in an hour," he beamed and watched her go until she was out of sight. He got up and brushed off his own clothes, walking into the cabin and into the kitchen – Eggos again it would be.

~

Shane and Kelsey had had absolutely no luck locating a den of any sort. They'd found a couple of what they presumed to be foxholes, but nothing that was nearly big enough to house a human-sized creature. After a couple of hours, Shane had collapsed on the ground, dejected and exhausted.

"Kelsey, what are we doing out here?" he asked, guzzling water.

"Looking for your monster... I thought that was what you wanted," she replied.

Shane shook his head, "It's just another dead end... Just like everything else." He looked up at her, the defeat visible in his eyes. "Are there any caves around here?"

"Not for several miles; definitely none that would be considered to be on Lake Vautour."

"Of course there aren't," Shane said disdainfully.

"Hey," Kelsey sat down next to him on the ground and rubbed his shoulders. "I am doing my best here: my best to keep an open mind and to think of ways to get to the bottom of this."

Shane looked at her and puffed out his cheeks, "I know. And I appreciate it. I'm just trying to wrap my head around how nothing I've tried has panned out. Like you said: it has to go *somewhere* when it's not out running around and hunting!"

Kelsey bit her lower lip, nodding. A smile slowly spread across her face. "How about we call it quits for today, huh? Go back to my house and sit out on the boat or drink 'virgin' mimosas? It'll give us a chance to clear our heads and just enjoy being together." Her smile wavered, "Because as much as I wanna help you find this thing, I also still wanna have some fun spending time together."

Shane looked around at the trees surrounding them and then back at Kelsey's face. "Kelsey... What is this?"

"What do you mean?"

"This... between us. What exactly is this?"

Kelsey bit her lower lip again, brushing the back of Shane's hand with her fingertips. "Whatever we want it to be, I guess."

"And what do you want it to be?" Shane asked, feeling like she was dancing around the point.

"I don't know," she stated. "I like you, Shane, but you're leaving at the end of the summer. Let's just... see where it takes us. Like I said: just enjoy some of the time that we do have."

"All right," he said, knowing that at least for now, he wasn't going to get a more definitive answer out of her. He had to admit that he'd been having similar thoughts; he really liked Kelsey, but he was leaving in the not-so-distant future. But who was to say that he wouldn't be back? Shane stood, helping Kelsey to her feet, and the two headed in the direction of the nearest trail.

~

Shane stopped outside of the ranger station. He looked around, getting the courage to go inside and confront Ranger Elton. He wasn't looking forward to being belittled and derided further, but he also had a point to make. Plus, he was sure that Ranger Elton had stolen his camera – well, Greg's camera, but what difference did it make? He took a deep breath and walked through the front door.

Ranger Elton was moving around behind the counter, obviously busy with something – or trying to look busy. He looked up as the door opened and noticed Shane, a look of recognition passing over his eyes, and he smirked, huffing out his nostrils.

"Shane Lucas, to what do I owe the pleasure? Want to report seeing the Loch Ness Monster in the lake? Or maybe Bigfoot?" Shane did his best to ignore his condescending words and tone. "Because if that is the case, I'm very busy with *real* things that need my attention."

"No, nothing like that," Shane said flatly, leaning on the counter. "I was wondering if there has been any sign of Ranger Damon, actually."

Ranger Elton paused briefly, but continued moving the boxes that he was organizing. He quickly resumed what he was doing, "No. I have contacted local authorities, and they're looking into it. Not really my problem anymore, except for the part where I have to do all his fucking work."

Shane tapped his fingers nervously on the counter before asking his next question, "… What about Greg Sanford?"

Ranger Elton actually stopped what he was doing and whipped around to stare at Shane, his eyes ablaze and the rest of his face contorted in a scowl. "For the last time," he practically growled, "Greg Sanford left of his own accord. Mystery solved. Don't you have better things to do than being here asking me all these questions? Doesn't Kelsey have something for you to be doing?"

For the first time since he arrived, Shane actually felt angry, "What business is that of yours?"

Ranger Elton scoffed, smirking and eyeing Shane. The smirk remained on his lips as he spoke, but his tone had grown serious, "Everything that goes on at Lake Vautour is my business. And you would do well to remember that."

"Like Hoodoo Joe?"

Ranger Elton's smirk disappeared, "What about him? He hasn't been bothering you or your parents?"

"No. But he told me he saw Greg
Sanford in the woods before he
disappeared–"

"Left," Ranger Elton interrupted him;
Shane ignored him, and continued.

"And he said he looked like he was
running from something."

Ranger Elton and Shane stared at each
other for a long moment, the clock on the
wall's second hand ticking the only sound.
Finally, Ranger Elton spoke, "That old
hermit is crazy. I wouldn't put stock in
anything he says. And stay away from
him."

"I thought you said he was harmless."

"He is; but there's no point bothering
him or riling him up. He leaves everyone
else alone, they leave him alone. Easy
arrangement. Now, do the same for me;
leave me alone to my work and go about
your day. Because no matter how much we
may dislike each other, we are both staying
here on the lake, and we have to exist in
roughly the same space. The less I see of

you, the better. And I definitely don't want to see you up here again wasting my time asking questions about that Goddamn nature photographer who just decided to go home. And that goes for phone calls too. I'm sure that you can find something better to do." He narrowed his eyes at Shane and then returned to his boxes.

Shane wanted to mention the camera, but decided that he had said enough. After all, Ranger Elton was right; for the time being, they did have to exist in the same area. As he exited the ranger station, he tried to figure out why Rosco admired the man so much. It was not just that he'd grown up around him so he was used to him; if that were the case, Kelsey would not hate him as much as she did. It was just another of Lake Vautour's many mysteries.

Shane turned and looked at the bulletin board. He saw that most of the missing flyers had been taken down. Shane wondered whether they had been found or the owners had just given up. There was a flyer up for Ranger Damon, with his photo and the phone number for the ranger station to call if you had any information concerning his whereabouts.

Shane smirked; he had information, but Ranger Elton refused to accept it. Shane grew a little glum; it really didn't make much difference for Ranger Damon whether or not Ranger Elton did anything with Shane's claims, since Shane was almost positive that his body was among the remains he'd seen in the carcass piles. What did concern him was the creature and who else it could hurt if nothing was done about it.

Chapter 14

Shane was awakened by the sound of something hitting his window. He lay in bed and listened. A few seconds passed before it happened again. He threw off the covers and swung his legs over the side of the bed, walking over to the window. On the lawn, he could make out Kelsey standing in the moonlight and holding something. He sighed, waving to acknowledge that he'd seen her. He quickly pulled on some clothes and walked quietly down the stairs to the back door to meet her.

"Kelsey, it's almost midnight, and I've told you that I don't like for you to be wandering around at night with that thing—"

"I heard something!" she cut him off excitedly, pulling him out the door and closing it behind him so that his parents would be less likely to hear them. He noticed that the item he had seen her holding was a baseball bat.

"You did?" Shane asked, all of the hairs on his body standing on end.

"Yeah. This weird… howl or scream, I don't know. I think I've heard it before actually, just didn't pay it much mind since it was across the lake. Just thought it was sound distortion in the night. But this time, I was listening for it. Come on, let's go," she grabbed his wrist, pulling him toward the trees.

"Whoa, whoa, whoa – no," Shane pulled free of her grasp, stepping back toward the cabin.

Kelsey pouted, giving him her best puppy dog eyes, "Shane…" She lifted the baseball bat in her hand.

"I am not going out there at night again," he said, suddenly sick to his stomach. "I'll drive you home; we shouldn't be out here."

"Come on! You went to investigate when you heard it, and all you had with you was a lousy flashlight."

"And I saw it attack, and presumably kill, Ranger Damon," Shane shot back. "I'm lucky it didn't attack me too. And it was a heavy duty flashlight."

"We'll be careful. We can stick to the trails and run back if things get dicey." She looked at Shane persuasively, "Seeing is believing. And don't you want me to believe you?"

Shane looked back at her uneasily. "… I can't. Not again." He turned and gripped the back door's handle.

"Well, I'm going either way. So, you can come with me or not." He looked back over his shoulder to see her glaring at him unwaveringly, her arms crossed over her chest.

"That bat won't do much against it," he tried to reason.

"You haven't seen my swing. I was on the softball team for a year, but then I got bored of it and quit."

Shane reluctantly walked over next to her, looking at her seriously. "Okay. It looks like I don't have a choice because I can't let you go out there by yourself. But you have to promise that if things start to look bad, we will run back, straight here," he pointed at the cabin.

"Yeah, duh."

The pair started down the trail; Shane couldn't help but feel uneasy, but it also felt kind of good to have someone besides the resident crazy person taking him seriously; this just was not the approach he would've chosen.

They walked along the trails for what felt like forever, but Shane knew it couldn't have been that long; everything just looked the same at night. Suddenly, Shane and Kelsey both froze as they heard someone or something moving through the brush. Shane held out his arm to shield Kelsey, pushing her partially behind him, even if she was the one with the bat. He could hear her breathing in large, frightened gasps and wanted to hold her hand to comfort her, but also knew that he needed to have his hands free and ready to face whatever was coming for them through the trees.

Hoodoo Joe and Ranger Elton emerged from the trees, freezing when they spotted Shane and Kelsey. The two pairs stared at each other for several long moments in silence.

Finally, Shane broke the silence, stammering as he spoke, "Y-You two?"

Hoodoo Joe and Ranger Elton shared a glance, only taking their eyes off of the teens for a second. "Well, dis changes tings," Hoodoo Joe said quietly, looking directly over Shane's shoulder at Kelsey. Shane slowly turned to look at her and saw that she was holding his gaze and glaring at him scornfully.

Shane turned back to the hermit and ranger, "What is going on here…?"

"Shane, listen," Ranger Elton took a step forward, holding his hands in front of him entreatingly, his expression and tone the softest that Shane had ever witnessed.

"This is all just one big misunderstanding. You shouldn't be here."

"What does that mean? Wha-What are you two doing out here?" Shane asked suspiciously, not moving away from Kelsey.

"Shane, there are things... Things that outsiders cannot understand. Just leave now and go home and forget this ever happened."

"And what about Kelsey? I'm just supposed to leave her here? I don't think so."

Ranger Elton sighed, shifting his gaze to Kelsey, and then looking back at Shane.

"Shane! Run!" Kelsey shouted, suddenly bolting to the left.

Shane stood, frozen for a moment, processing, and then moved to follow her. Hoodoo Joe had also begun to follow her movement, much faster than Shane would've thought the old man was capable of moving, and grabbed her by the arm. She let out a scream, dropping the bat.

Shane lunged for him, holding up his fists, but Ranger Elton leapt between them.

"Hold off, Shane!" he shouted, both authoritatively and pleadingly, and Shane stopped, but kept his hands balled into fists, ready to fight.

Hoodoo Joe held firmly onto Kelsey's upper arm with one hand. Shane lunged again, but Ranger Elton held him back, gripping his shoulders. Kelsey began to cry, looking at Shane, a look of sheer terror in her eyes.

"Let me go!" Shane shouted, fighting against Ranger Elton's grasp.

"Please don't let them kill me, Shane!" Kelsey wept, sobbing.

"Shane, stop! You do not understand!" Ranger Elton cried, surprisingly strong for his small stature and age.

Hoodoo Joe retrieved a folding pocket knife from his pants' pocket with his free hand, pulling out the blade with his teeth and holding it to Kelsey's throat. "No! No, please! Don't kill me! Sacrifice him!" she pointed at Shane. "Give it Shane!" she begged.

Shane stopped fighting against Ranger Elton, staring at her, crushed; he felt equally shocked and as if he'd been stabbed in the chest. Hoodoo Joe and Ranger Elton looked at her in equal shock. After a long, tense silence, Hoodoo Joe began to laugh wheezily. "It doesn't want him! And besides, it's your time, anyway." He began to apply more pressure to the knife, and she let out a scream. "Don't worry," he cooed. "I'm not gonna slit your throat. Just need to let out enough blood to lure him to you."

She continued to sob, looking at Shane once more, "Shane… Please… Don't let them do this to me." Shane looked back at her, still in shock, no fight left in him. He was experiencing a flurry of emotions: shock, heartbreak, betrayal, anger. He didn't know what to do; he was in a total daze.

Hoodoo Joe looked at Shane seriously, speaking in a low tone, "Help us, Shane. If you help dis thing, it leaves you alone."

Shane felt a lump form in his throat, and he had to fight back the urge to vomit. Hoodoo Joe had lied to him… He did know about the creature – not only knew about it, but was killing for it, possibly even Ranger Damon and Greg Sanford. And Ranger Elton was in on it too.

"Shane, it's a lie; don't listen to him!" Kelsey screamed, trying to choke down her sobs. "I helped, and look at where I am now."

Hoodoo Joe let out another wheezy guffaw, "You never 'helped!' You just threw othas unda the bus. Like your parents; remember dat, *cher*?"

Kelsey laughed in disbelief, shaking her head, but being careful not to brush up against Hoodoo Joe's knife.

"N-No," Shane finally found his voice, looking between Hoodoo Joe and Ranger Elton. "Rosco told me what happened. It was an accident; they lost control of the car in the fog."

Ranger Elton sighed heavily, "No… We made it look that way." He closed his eyes and pinched the bridge of nose; remembering what had happened seemed to bring him much pain. "Joe called me… He'd heard the crash. When I got there and found the car, the front doors were literally torn off their hinges and the windshield was smashed. Blood was everywhere, and neither of them were anywhere to be seen. I walked a little ways into the trees and found them… or at least, what was left.

"When I went back to the car, I found that the brake lines had been cut. It didn't take me long to figure out what had happened; I knew they had been having a lot of trouble with Kelsey around that time, and she was the only other person beside Joe and myself who knew about what lurks in these woods. What better way to get what she wanted than to let it do her dirty work?" Ranger Elton looked up at Kelsey, narrowing his eyes.

"It's not true! I had nothing to do with it!" she vehemently denied, fresh tears rolling down her cheeks.

"I did what I could to make it look like an accident; had my work cut out for me so that the other investigators wouldn't find the cut brake line." He continued to look at Kelsey, shaking his head, "I covered for you."

"Who are you kidding; you covered for yourself, you lousy jerk," she spat, kicking Hoodoo Joe in the knee and causing him to collapse. He threw out his arms, letting out a cry of agony as he hit the ground, and Kelsey took off running.

"Shit!" Ranger Elton rushed to Hoodoo Joe.

Shane took off after Kelsey, his feet pounding on the ground as he struggled to catch up to her. Once he caught up to her, they were both breathing heavily, but refused to slow down.

"What the hell was that back there?" he asked, panting. "You've known this whole time!?"

"I couldn't just tell you; we were all sworn to secrecy. I finally had to start acting like I was open to the idea of a creature when you weren't gonna talk to me anymore. You weren't *supposed* to find out about it."

"You told them to kill me... You were willing to offer me up to save yourself..." Shane said, hurt; he'd thought that they really had something, but now he was questioning everything that had happened between them since he'd arrived at Lake Vautour.

"It was all a ruse to help us escape," she explained. "If they thought I was on their side, they would let me go. Then, when they were trying to get ahold of you, we could both make a run for it."

Shane wanted to believe her more than anything, but he was skeptical, especially after hearing what the two men had to say.

He did not know who or what to believe anymore.

Kelsey looked over at him and noticed the look of uncertainty on his face. "You don't believe me?"

Shane looked back at her, his heart aching, "Did you kill your parents?"

"What? No! I can't believe that you would even think that! They were trying to fill your head with lies, to get you on their side." The look of doubt remained on Shane's face and in his eyes. Kelsey shook her head scornfully, "You don't believe me. I hope it tears your whole family limb from limb."

Shane felt rage bubble up in his gut and envelop him, and he lunged at Kelsey, causing them both to lose their footing and tumble down the hill they'd been skirting.

Chapter 15

The two of them rolled down the hill,
Shane losing his sweaty grip on Kelsey.
They hit their arms and legs as they
tumbled, their ribs and backs already aching
before they ever reached the bottom; Shane
wrapped his arms around his head to protect
it and his neck. They hit the ground mere
yards from each other. They didn't bother
to catch their breath; they lunged at each
other. Kelsey tried to get her hands around
Shane's neck in a stranglehold, but Shane
gripped her wrists and pushed her arms
down to her sides, quickly overpowering
her. The two wrestled, but it was barely a
competition; Shane had her pinned on the
ground in seconds.

"What are you going to do?" Kelsey
scoffed, laughing derisively. "Kill m-
HRRK!" Shane cut her off as he wrapped
his hands around her throat, beginning to
choke her. She gagged, pulling at his wrists
as her eyes bulged and she struggled for air.

Not only had she tried to betray him, she had threatened his family.

"Shane, stop!" Ranger Elton's voice rang out from the top of the hill. Shane looked up to see that the two men had caught up and were making their way carefully down the hill to avoid losing their footing. "You are not a killer! Let the creature do its job, no one else has to get hurt – at least for a while." They had reached the bottom of the hill, "Help us, and we can make sure that your family stays safe."

Shane watched them carefully, still filled with rage and breathing heavily. He slowly loosened his grip, but kept Kelsey pinned, straddling her so that she couldn't run away. She breathed in a large breath and began coughing, bringing her hand up to her neck, tears streaming down the sides of her face as she caught her breath.

Ranger Elton and Hoodoo Joe walked closer, but kept a safe distance; they didn't want to make Shane feel cornered so he'd do something rash. "Well, there's no avoiding it now…" Ranger Elton said in obvious defeat. "We have some explaining to do."

"Yeah," Shane nodded, panting and sniffing; he was beginning to feel the pain from the fall as the adrenaline started to go out of his system – his scrapes stung and where he knew there would be bruises ached. "You do."

Ranger Elton took a deep breath and looked at Hoodoo Joe woefully before turning back to Shane, "Joe and I have been feeding it for years. Sometimes, the wildlife wasn't always enough to keep it at bay, and we needed to keep it from killing just anyone and anything."

Ranger Elton stared at the ground, stroking his beard. "It took my wife…" he said quietly. A long silence followed. "I spent years trying to find a way to send it back to whatever Hell it came from. But I couldn't… It is a part of the forest. It has been here since long before mankind walked this earth. So, since we can't kill it... we had to find a way to live with it and reduce the damage.

"I'm sure that this sounds morally wrong to you, and don't think I do not battle with myself internally about it. But we have no choice. We only feed it people when absolutely necessary – when its hunger won't be sated by animals, which only happens every few years – and even then, it's usually hitchhikers or squatters..."

"But what *is* it?" Shane asked, trying to process everything they were telling him.

"We call it the *Maci-Manetoowa*, which basically means 'mean spirit' in the tongue of the Native tribes that used to live here. They also called this land *Maci-Manetoowa Atahki*, which means 'land of the bad spirit.' Too bad the early settlers didn't know that."

"So... So you help it kill people?" Shane said is disgust.

Ranger Elton stroked his beard, sighing heavily, "It's either that or let it kill who, when, and where it pleases. Do not think I have stopped looking for a way to get rid of it… But there just doesn't seem to be one."

"So, we made an arrangement," Hoodoo Joe spoke for the first time since they had arrived. "I'd stay in da woods to keep an eye on tings, as I had for years before Elton eva came on da scene."

"And I would monitor things from a more official perspective and try to keep it out of the public eye," Ranger Elton resumed his explanation. "We did a pretty good job of going undetected until about five years ago, when Kelsey caught us in the act. There was no denying what we were doing; we were carrying the body of a hitchhiker Joe had clobbered to leave out for it. We had to explain ourselves: that we were feeding a creature that was a part of the woods and by doing so, maintaining the peace and safety of those living around the lake.

"She took it pretty well for a girl her age. She asked if she could be included, help us out if we needed it. If we did, she wouldn't tell. So, that only left us with two choices… *one* choice really. We had to include her, which sure beat the alternative, since we could not risk being found out." Ranger Elton looked grimly at Shane, and he did not have to explain what he meant.

"And things went smoothly, surprisingly smooth, until she killed her parents. That was not part of the deal," he glared at Kelsey, and she shot him a dirty look and let out a light cough. "Not only were her parents not part of our deal, given that our goal was to protect those living around the lake, it was not even necessary to sacrifice anyone at the time… It was sated. After that, we kept a much closer eye on her and what she was up to. Rosco is a good man. I almost view him as my own son. I care and fear for him."

Kelsey let out a patronizing laugh, causing her to cough again. Once she'd recovered, she looked at Ranger Elton and Hoodoo Joe, a wicked smile on her face, "If you care about Rosco so much, why are you trying to kill his kid sister?"

"Because you're a psychopath and would eventually kill him too!" Ranger Elton spat, pointing at her accusingly. "I know that you are responsible for Damon's death. That was the last straw. After your parents, we just tightened your leash, but we let you live so that Rosco would not lose *everyone*. But after you killed Damon, you only confirmed for us that if people get close to you, they die, because you see this as a game."

"I had nothing to do with that," Kelsey said defiantly, gritting her teeth.

"Bullshit, we all know better. You literally just finished trying to offer up Shane to save your skin."

Kelsey glared at him, her eyes burning with contempt; if looks could kill, this one would have. "And what about Greg Sanford? I know *you* are responsible for his disappearance. So I guess that makes you a hypocrite." Ranger Elton said

nothing, but Shane noticed that he'd
tightened his jaw. "I saw you carving those
symbols in the trees," she snickered.

"Yeah – I was doing what I could
while we tried to figure things out."

Kelsey rolled her eyes, "And I'm not
stupid; I know that you were grooming
Damon to take your place. After all, you
are getting old – too old to be doing this
very much longer." She sniffed, seeming to
be fighting back angry tears, "That was
supposed to be *my* place!"

"You know what, yeah, you're right; I
was trying out Damon to take my place, but
that did not mean you were out. Joe will
need a replacement too." Hoodoo Joe
nodded silently. Ranger Elton shook his
head sorrowfully, "You could've had him,
you know? You and Damon could've been
quite the pair, a real power couple. I'd seen
the way you two looked at each other, the
way you acted. I just needed someone who
both knew the woods and had the ranger

authority." Ranger Elton continued to shake his head.

"The creature was hungry; I took care of it," she said defiantly.

"But that's not how this works! We are supposed to protect our own; that's the whole point!" Ranger Elton shot back.

"Sorry I killed your protégé," Kelsey retorted mockingly.

Shane's eyes widened; she had confessed, and despite everything, he was shocked to hear her say it. Ranger Elton glowered at her, but said nothing; it was clear to see from the way he talked about Ranger Damon and the look in his eyes that he was still grieving the loss. Hoodoo Joe watched his partner, an angry sneer coming across his face. He had a look in his eyes that Shane had never seen there before – the look of a hunter.

He pulled out his knife and started toward Shane and Kelsey. Shane scrambled off of Kelsey as the knife-wielding hermit continued to advance, once again at surprising speed. Shane fell on his backside and continued to scoot backwards, crushing twigs and leaves under his palms as he did so. Kelsey braced her arms against the ground to get up, but Hoodoo Joe was already upon her and buried his knife in the side of her gut.

She let out a scream of pain, falling flat on her back again as Hoodoo Joe removed his knife, the blade stained dark red with blood. She continued to let out small cries as she put her hand over the wound, trying to stop the pain and bleeding. Hoodoo Joe quickly wiped his blade on the grass and folded it closed, replacing it in his pocket. Both he and Ranger Elton approached Shane as he stared at Kelsey in astonishment; a piece of him still wanted to help her as he watched her lying there, wincing in pain and injured.

The yowl of the *Maci-Manetoowa* pulled him back to reality, and he looked up at Ranger Elton and Hoodoo Joe as they each gripped one of his arms and pulled him to his feet. His knees were weak, and he hurt all over, but he managed to stand with their help.

"Come with us now," Hoodoo Joe urged Shane, staring at him. "You do not want to witness what is gonna happen to her."

Kelsey tried to push herself up with her leg, but gave up, whimpering in agony.

"Do-Does she have to d–" Shane started to ask, but another yowl cut through the air, closer this time.

"We *have* to go," Ranger Elton said firmly, pulling Shane toward the hill, which would take them back to the path.

Reluctantly, he followed. Once they were up the hill and had made their way through the trees so that they were back on the path, they picked up the pace, heading back toward the lake. As they neared the canoe launch, they could see the full moon reflecting off of the water through the trees.

They heard something crashing through the trees ahead of them to their left

– something that was very big and moving very fast. The creature emerged, running past them on all fours. It barely spared them a glance as it ran toward its prey. Ranger Elton and Hoodoo Joe seemed undisturbed by the brief encounter, but Shane had still felt his heart skip a beat as it had run past. Perhaps it was because this was not their first encounter with it, or perhaps it was because they knew that it would not bother them since it was hunting something else.

Kelsey gripped her side, crying out in pain as she tried to sit up so that she could stand. It hurt too much to bend her abdomen, so she laid back down and rolled over, digging the fingers of her free hand into the dirt. She'd heard the yowl, as she'd heard it many nights for her whole life; for the past few years, she'd known what it meant. She did not want to – could not – let it catch her.

She spotted a tree a couple of yards away with a low hanging branch. She began to drag herself across the ground toward it. She quickly realized that she was moving too slow only using one arm and had to release her side so that she could use both of them while pushing with her legs. Her hand was soaked with blood, as was her shirt and the waistband of her shorts; she could feel it flowing out of the open wound, leaving a trail behind her as she hauled herself toward the tree.

She could hear the creature approaching, its feet pounding on the ground and the snapping of branches, not to mention the yowls. If she could just get to her feet, she could run…

Fuck them; fuck all of them. Fuck Elton and Hoodoo Joe. Fuck Damon, but she had already made that point. And fuck Shane Lucas – his parents she merely lumped in with him.

She winced as a twig poked her wound and stifled a cry, spitting up a little blood.

She arched her neck to see how close she was to the tree. It was only a few feet away, and while she would have to really stretch, she was sure that she could reach it. The creature yowled again, a terrible, eager hunting cry; it was even closer now. She had to get to her feet.

She took a few deep breaths, filling her lungs with air. She dragged herself the few feet to the foot of the tree and leaned her forehead against it. She looked up and reached for the branch. Her hand grasped empty air. She swiped again and missed. She took a deep breath and pushed herself up along the trunk and stretched, reaching again. She heard the creature crest and begin down the hill, yowling as it spotted her.

Her fingers closed around the rough branch. She smiled, letting out a small laugh of triumph. She heaved her other arm up and gripped the branch with both hands and pulled. Just as she stood, trying to get her legs steady before releasing the branch, the creature leapt upon her, gripping her shoulders, its claws digging into her shoulders and neck, and burying its fangs into her bleeding side.

Kelsey's screams echoed through the trees, and Shane paused, breathing heavily and looking between Ranger Elton and Hoodoo Joe. They both nodded sadly; no words were needed. They all knew what had happened as the screams ceased and silence followed.

Shane looked at the ground, fighting tears and the urge to hyperventilate; he was a flurry of emotions, and while in some ways this felt like a terrible nightmare, it was also far too real: the aching he felt all over, the coating of sweat on his skin and his hair, the constant churning of his stomach. He knew he was going to wake up in the morning with his new knowledge and that Kelsey would not be coming around to knock at the back door.

The trio walked the rest of the way to the trail that led out to Shane's family's cabin. When they reached the trailhead, Shane turned to face them. "So… That's it then?"

"That's it then," Ranger Elton said, setting his mouth in a firm line and giving a curt nod. "It's best not to say anything about this to anyone – especially your parents and Rosco. We will talk to you soon."

Shane nodded; even if he'd wanted to tell someone, he wasn't sure that he could. And if past experience was any indicator, they wouldn't believe him anyway.

Hoodoo Joe sighed, removing his hat and scratching the top of his mostly bald head. "I am so sorry dat you had to get involved. I did my best to steer you away from da truth; to convince you dat dere was nothin' to see, especially after you saw da creature attack and kill Ranger Damon and found dat camera."

Shane turned toward the cabin, but then faced the two men again, "One more thing. Kelsey said that you were responsible for Greg Sanford disappearing?… Is that true?" He looked directly at Ranger Elton.

"I didn't have to do anything; he got too close to it on his own," Ranger Elton replied.

"Then why did you steal the camera?"

"As I said, it's my job to keep things under wraps. I was looking for anything of his that day I saw you in the woods. I figured out that you'd lied to me about the camera, so I made an excuse to get in the house." Ranger Elton fixed his gaze on Shane; he had a new expression that Shane hadn't seen there before, almost like admiration, "You're a smart kid, Shane. A little too smart for your own good." A small smile tugged at the corner of his mouth for a fraction of a second. "But a lot has happened tonight. You have a lot to process. Get some sleep; we'll talk soon."

He patted Shane's shoulder, and Hoodoo Joe tipped his hat to him before they both turned and headed back down the trail.

Shane watched them go and then turned back to the cabin. It stood on the hill, looking out over the seemingly peaceful lake. Shane started back. He knew that nothing would – *could* – ever be the same after what he had seen and what he knew. He agonized over how he would be able to act normal around his parents. And he knew that he could not avoid Rosco forever; nor did he really want to. But lying to him would be even harder. He wondered if Rosco had any inkling of what his sister was truly like... She'd sure had the wool pulled over Shane's eyes.

Shane opened and closed the back door carefully so as not to make any noise and locked it behind him. He crept up the stairs to his room and changed out of his clothes, dropping them on the floor. He went into the bathroom on the first floor and took a quick shower to clean out his cuts and wash off the dirt. Once he dried off and put on his pajamas, he laid down in his bed, his hair still damp. He couldn't close his eyes; every time he did, images of the creature and the night's events played out behind his eyelids. He did not feel sleepy at all, despite being utterly exhausted. He hoped that some night he would be able to sleep again, but tonight would not be that night.

Chapter 16

A few weeks passed, and still, Kelsey Ewan was missing. Summer vacation was nearly over, so Shane and his family had already started packing up some things that they weren't using to make it easier for them to load the car when the day came to head back to St. Louis. In theory, they could stay a little longer, but Shane's parents wanted him to have a chance to acclimate back to being home in the city after spending all summer at the lake. They had no idea just *how* necessary that really was.

Shane had finally managed to fall asleep sometime in the wee hours of the night it had all gone to Hell. He'd awakened to the birds tweeting and the sounds of his mother cooking breakfast in the kitchen downstairs. Everything seemed as it had been, but Shane knew that it wasn't. Or perhaps rather everything *was* as it had been, but he was just seeing everything through new eyes.

He'd half expected Kelsey to come skipping up to the house, all smiles and ready for an escapade or to go monster hunting, to realize that it really all had been some twisted nightmare, but his gut and heart told him differently.

All of that was confirmed later that evening when a car came speeding up the driveway to the cabin like a bat out of Hell. It was Rosco, and he was in a panic; he was used to not seeing Kelsey during the day, but she was always back by dinnertime, and he had seen no sign of her. He'd driven over to the Lucases' cabin in hopes that she was there and had just forgotten to tell him.

Of course, she hadn't been there, and Shane had done his best to avoid having to talk to Rosco; he'd let his parents handle all of that for now. He was still too busy processing everything: The creature, or *Maci-Manetoowa,* as Ranger Elton and Hoodoo Joe called it. That the two of them were basically in league with it, for a supposed greater good. That Kelsey had been a part of it all as well, but gone rogue and basically murdered Ranger Damon and her parents. That she'd been lying to him all summer… He wondered just how much of their time together had been all lies. But all things considered, he was in no state to put on a façade for Rosco.

After not finding her at the Lucases', Rosco had gone up to the ranger station and reported her missing to Ranger Elton and then called the local authorities. Of course, they could not list her as officially missing until forty-eight hours passed. When she didn't turn up, flyers had gone up, and a search party had been organized; of course, Ranger Elton had taken care of disbanding it and managing the legwork himself.

During that time, Shane had been approached by Ranger Elton and Hoodoo Joe. They told him that they were sure that Kelsey had lured him out into the woods with her that night as insurance since she was fairly certain that the two of them were plotting against her when they had called a midnight meeting. Having him there would make it so that their hands were tied, or the other tactic she had tried, they would have to get him out of the way to keep him quiet, opening a window for her to make her escape.

They had also told him that he was a part of it now, whether or not any of them liked it. He had to keep the secret and put up the façade that everything was fine. When Shane had asked how they managed to keep up the charade, Ranger Elton had answered, "Just be a mean asshole all the time."

"Or let everyone think you're a kook," Hoodoo Joe had added.

Shane opted for a third option; he would not offer more than was asked of him, and if he ever was asked directly, he'd just shrug it off as silliness. Ranger Elton assured him that everything with Kelsey had been taken care of; no one would be able to find out what had really happened. As far as anyone was concerned, she had run off and hitched a ride to anywhere. Or at least, that was what he'd told Rosco had likely happened, though he also assured him that they were doing everything they could to track her down.

In Kelsey's absence, Shane had been spending a lot of time with Rosco. Once he had come to terms with everything – at least, as well as he was going to – he felt like it was the right thing to do. After all, Rosco was all alone in that big house that he'd shared with family for his whole life. And Shane had nothing better to be doing; he would no longer be hiking with Kelsey, or really on his own, for that matter.

Rosco seemed to enjoy the company, and after the first week passed by with no sign of Kelsey, he had begun to accept that she probably wasn't coming back. One day, while he and Shane sat out on the patio sipping beers, he'd turned to Shane and said, "I'm sad that she's gone, but if I'm being honest, I'm not entirely surprised. While we were all the other had after our parents died, she always seemed to want more than what was here. She wanted a grander life with more going on. I guess I just didn't expect her to leave so soon or without saying good-bye." He swirled his beer and took a large drink. "Figured she would leave for college and then make a permanent move; then at least I'd have somewhere to visit or send mail to."

Shane nodded quietly, staring down into his beer. A piece of him felt terrible for lying to Rosco; Shane had never been much of a liar, and typically when he did lie, he wasn't much good at it. His newfound penchant for lying was one of the many things that had changed about him, and he was not sure that he liked it.

But another part of him felt like maybe it really was for the best to let Rosco believe the lie. It was better than him knowing the truth: that his sister had killed their parents and Ranger Damon, tried to kill Shane, and then died at the claws of a creature older than mankind – plus that there was a strong likelihood that she would've eventually tried to kill him too. And maybe some good could come of it – maybe he could finally open the garage he'd dreamed of having for so many years.

When the night before Shane and his family were going to leave finally came, Shane was very sad to say good-bye to Rosco. He'd thought he was cool and enjoyed spending time with him before Kelsey had disappeared, but in the couple of weeks that followed, they had become quite close; he was the closest thing Shane had ever had to an older brother. Shane almost felt guilty for leaving, knowing that he'd be alone, still waiting to see if Kelsey would turn up or come back, and Shane knowing that she wouldn't.

They sat around the lit fire circle, listening to the crickets, an odd silence between them. Rosco had finally broken it, patting Shane's shoulder and saying, "Good luck with your senior year, man. I'm sure you will do great; you seem to have a good head on your shoulders."

"Thanks," Shane nodded. "Good luck with… everything."

Rosco grimaced, looking out over the lake and nodding. "It's, uh, going to be different, but I'll adjust. You going to be back next summer?"

Shane knew that his parents planned on coming back, and all things considered, he was sure that he would be too. "Yeah, probably. That's the plan, at least."

"Great. I'm sure I'll see you around then; be sure to come say hi when you get in. I may even have that garage up and running by then," he chuckled.

"Yeah, that'd be great."

The two talked a little longer, and then Rosco drove Shane back over to his cabin, and they said their final good-byes. Shane walked inside and couldn't help but feel terrible; Rosco was glad that he would be coming back, and he'd built practically all of their newfound friendship on lies, the very thing he had condemned Kelsey for doing to him.

The following morning while Shane's parents started packing the car, he was up in his room, finishing putting away last minute things. He opened the drawer of his desk and found the baggie with the ranger badge, the blood dried and deep maroon. There did not seem to be any point in keeping it now.

He brought all of his things downstairs and piled them in the front room, then went out the back door to put the baggie in the outdoor trashcan where his parents were less likely to see it; they rarely ever used the outdoor trashcan other than to put out the bags from inside, and even then, they never looked inside. As he lifted the lid and dropped it in, he noticed a movement along the tree line. He looked up and spotted Hoodoo Joe. The two locked eyes, and Hoodoo Joe gestured with his head for Shane to come over.

Shane looked around to make sure that his parents weren't paying attention and then headed for the trail. A little ways into the trees, he found Ranger Elton waiting as well.

"So, this is it," Ranger Elton said, looking at Shane seriously. "Remember our secret? The thing that binds us together?"

"How could I forget?" Shane harrumphed, looking between the two men.

Hoodoo Joe chuckled, "Da boy has a point. Just rememba: you cannot breathe a word of dis to anotha livin' soul."

Shane sighed, "I won't. Not like anyone would believe me, anyway."

"Once again, da boy has a point. I like dis one," Hoodoo Joe laughed, crossing his arms and smiling at Ranger Elton.

Ranger Elton gave a slight nod, but did not smile or laugh. "Shane, we have been doing some thinking and some talking… What we said that night about Joe and me getting older, it still is a hard truth. We will need someone to take over when we're gone – someone we can trust. You're a much better person than Kelsey ever was; we added her to our little… 'group' out of necessity. She was a bad apple; we should've known that when she was so eager to help. But you're a good person; you wouldn't just kill people because you can."

Shane looked at them seriously, his guts twisting up into knots, "I don't know… That is a lot to ask."

"Believe me, we know that," Ranger Elton said sympathetically.

"But we also feel confident in our decision… Dis time," Hoodoo Joe added.

Shane dropped his gaze to the ground, a battle of morals storming inside him. He knew that in a way, if he did this, he would be playing a crucial role in protecting his family, Rosco, and others around the lake. But, even if it wasn't every year, he would have to leave people out for it to eat, which in his eyes was still no different than if he'd killed them himself. Then again, did he really have a choice, given his new knowledge?

"I know why you're hesitant," Ranger Elton said, taking a few steps toward him. "I was too when Joe first told me what would be necessary to prevent it from taking someone else like it did my wife. But there are just some forces in the universe that you can't reckon with; you just have to appease them in the interest of the greater good. It's lousy, but that's just the way life works sometimes."

Hoodoo Joe chimed in, "And you said it yourself; your parents would neva believe you. Say when Elton and I are gone, your parents still want to come back. Who is to say dat it doesn't kill dem den, with nobody to keep it in check?"

Shane felt a lump form in his throat. He hated it, but they had a point; he would never be able to come up with a way to make his parents give up the cabin, even with his newfound penchant for lying.

"I know you have what it takes," Ranger Elton said in an even, yet dominating, tone. "When I took the camera, I saw your map. You already have an understanding of these woods. Add to that your knowledge of the truth and your moral compass, and you are the best candidate to come our way since Damon."

"Betta, even," Hoodoo Joe said, and Ranger Elton shot him a scowl.

Shane looked up at Ranger Elton, his heart pounding in his chest, "Maybe I'm not as good as you think. I would've killed Kelsey that night if you two hadn't intervened. I didn't know I had that in me, but when she threatened my family, I just… went over the edge."

"Precisely," Ranger Elton replied. "We stand by what we said."

"After all, look at your motives. You were just tryin' to protect da people dat you love," Hoodoo Joe added.

"What do you say, Shane? Help us out?" Ranger Elton asked. "As much as you may want things to be, they can never be 'normal' again, no matter where you go or what you do."

Shane looked up at them, and a sad smile tugged at one side of his mouth as he nodded knowingly. "I'll see you next summer," he said, his voice wavering just a little.

"Yes, you will, *cher*," Hoodoo Joe said, tipping his hat.

"Have a good school year," Ranger Elton said, and Shane turned to walk back up to the cabin.

"Hey, where were you?" Don asked as Shane came in the back door. "We went up to your room, and you weren't there. Is this all your stuff?" He indicated the things Shane had piled in the front room.

"Yeah, that's all. I was just making sure I hadn't left anything out back," Shane replied.

"Well, I hope you have everything because we're about to ship out," Don began to pick up Shane's things, then stood and turned back into the cabin, looking around and resting his hands on his hips. "Sure am going to miss this place... Your mom and I are thinking of buying something similar when we retire. Can't wait to come back next summer." He bent and picked up one of Shane's bags. "Come on, help me get these out to the car; it's a long drive ahead of us."

Shane nodded and walked over to help his dad put his things in the car. As they were loading, Don looked at Shane, a thoughtful expression on his face. "It's still so weird that your friend ran off like that. I wouldn't have ever expected her to do anything like that; she seemed to love the woods and got along well with her brother."

"Yeah," Shane said dismissively.

Don noticed his dismissiveness and took it as a sign that he did not want to talk about it, in which case, he was right. "Oh well, there will be other girls," he grinned reassuringly and closed the back gate.

The two climbed into the car where Beth was already settled and waiting on them. Shane stared out the window as they drove away, watching Lake Vautour disappear behind the cover of trees. The summer had brought a lot of changes: his first love, countless adventures, new friends – or rather – partners, and a dark secret. Lake Vautour had proven to be anything but boring. He only wondered what stories he'd tell his friends back home – which ones that were true, at least.

About the Author

Sarah J Dhue is a fiction author from Illinois and has been writing since she was in elementary school. She self-publishes her creative fiction, and this is her twelfth published book to date, as well as her fourth time completing a NaNoWriMo novel. She loves networking with other writers – and artists of other media – and runs a writing group that meets weekly. Some of her other interests include coffee, photography, graphic design, social media, animation, animals, art, travel, and music. Sarah currently resides with her family and cats in southern Illinois.

To learn more about Sarah, visit sarahjdhuephotos.com